FATHERS,
SONS & GOLF

FATHERS, SONS & GOLF

LESSONS IN HONOR AND INTEGRITY

ANDREW SHANLEY

HYPERION

NEW YORK

Library of Congress Cataloging-in-Publication Data

ISBN 0-7868-6245-9

Book design by Claudyne Bianco Bedell

FIRST EDITION

10 9 8 7 6 5 4 3 2 1

FOR MY FATHER AND MOTHER,

JOE AND ELAINE SHANLEY

*

CONTENTS

INTRODUCTION   1

1. BEGINNING WITH APPRECIATION   21

2. SWINGING AWAY   41

3. PAYING ATTENTION   73

4. CONNECTING THE MIND AND BODY   93

5. PLAYING TOGETHER   117

6. IN THE GROOVE   143

CONTENTS

7. TEACHING OUR CHILDREN WELL   **167**

8. IN THE NAME OF THE FATHER, SON,
AND HOLY SPIRIT   **193**

9. THE PROMISE OF REDEMPTION   **213**

FATHERS,
SONS & GOLF

I can't recall how or when I determined it was time for my two sons to earn an allowance, do their own gift shopping, or make significant decisions for themselves. I do, however, have a vivid recollection of the moment I knew it was time to teach them the game of golf.

It was a Sunday afternoon in late winter. As had become my custom, I had snuck off alone to watch golf on television. This habit, which had developed with quiet momentum over the past year, was benign as habits go, but it was a habit, nevertheless, and one about which I was secretive. Typically, I might not complete more than a dozen rounds of golf a year, and yet I hardly missed an afternoon of Sunday television golf. I was embarrassed by this, in general considering myself a doer, not a watcher.

I was also aware that most people considered viewing golf on television tedious. But this was my *Masterpiece Theater*, with adventure as dramatic as the story of Apollo 13: the man atop the leader board, his desire to claim the title sucking the oxygen from his atmosphere, needing somehow to get back home to the clubhouse, the heat shield blown apart, hands struggling to grip the controls.

I must also admit that I kept this habit of watching golf to myself as much out of a desire not to share it. This was my time to stoke up the competitive fires and feel them burning, and witness the drive in other men to excel at their chosen calling. It reminded me that I never wanted to give up the good fight, and that I, too, had a considerable need to experience accomplishment. These few hours as a spectator helped keep me in touch with such powerful emotions and resolutions.

On that particular Sunday afternoon I was also rewarded for my devotion to the game in a way so significant and so lasting that I believe it entirely explains and certainly justifies all the time I'd spent in front of the television.

INTRODUCTION

I was sitting there in my comfortable stuffed chair as the announcer alerted the audience that the next installment of the feature "Golf, the Great Game of Honor" was coming up shortly. I had seen a few of the previous segments, a series of episodes in golfing history in which individual golfers demonstrated unusual integrity. I knew, too, on that fateful afternoon that I wanted my sons to be exposed to this type of demonstration.

I immediately called out to Colin, aged thirteen, and McLean, aged ten. I could hear them out in the kitchen, fighting with each other over who had rights to the last pizza in the freezer. I raised my voice, asking them to come quickly to watch something on television with me.

When they saw it was golf, they both hesitated at the door. "It's coming up in a second," I said, motioning them to take a seat on the couch behind me. I didn't offer any explanation or introduction, assuming the segment would speak for itself.

We watched together as "Golf, the Great Game of Honor" recalled the 1983 British Open and Hale Irwin's loss of that prestigious championship. Irwin had called a stroke penalty on himself after he took a careless swipe at a two-inch putt, missing it altogether, before tapping it into the hole. Though he might have gotten away with this transgression, Irwin knew what he had done, and that was all that mattered. He called the penalty and later finished a single shot behind the leader.

When the segment ended, I turned to face my sons. "Pretty cool that he did that, huh?" I asked casually. So public a demonstration of integrity was remarkably rare, and I found it deeply moving. I admired the courage underlying it, and I felt the weight of its loneliness. In a world in which we have to struggle constantly against the odds merely to make our way, the decision to voluntarily accept a penalty can seem to diminish the very chance of survival. We can hardly keep from trembling when confronted by such integrity.

I've always been particularly vulnerable to these uncommon acts of character when my own emotions are bubbling up at the surface. This was certainly one of those times. We'd just learned that my wife, Karen, was pregnant. I couldn't believe my luck. At age forty-three, I would be a father again, able to relive what had been the most satisfying and joyful experience of my life. To find myself at the start all over again—well, it was even better than the first time, for now it was absent the anxiety over exploring the unknown. I knew that, except for the late-night duty, I would revel in the role.

But as I turned to see the boys' reaction, it was painfully clear to me that Colin and McLean did not tremble at the sight of Hale Irwin's honesty. Actually, they had no reaction at all.

Initially, this lack of response left me startled and confused. It hadn't occurred to me that my sons wouldn't naturally feel pride at seeing one of their species show of what strong and noble stuff we are really made.

But as I began to consider their apparent indifference, my bewilderment edged towards panic. "Were you watching?" I asked. "Do you understand what they just showed us?"

"Yes," they both said, a little perplexed by the force behind my question.

But in this case, I knew, understanding wasn't achieved without a depth of feeling accompanying it. My boys had not felt weak, and then felt their spirits soar.

Making a perfunctory nod in their direction, I turned back to stare blankly at the television screen as Colin and McLean silently left the room.

I lapsed into self-recrimination. While I knew myself to be a good and conscientious father, I'd clearly been negligent in passing on some quite fundamental values. This was my second wake-up call in less than two weeks.

The week before, McLean and I had been talking at dinner about kids who cheated on tests in school. I'd asked him if he'd ever cheated.

"Not really," McLean answered, pushing his food around his plate distractedly.

"What do you mean, not really?" I asked.

"Well, it's not really cheating if you aren't really trying to look when you see the answer on somebody else's paper."

"Why isn't that cheating?"

"Because you weren't really looking for the answer, and because you might have remembered the answer anyway. You might have figured it out on your own anyway."

"Yes, but you didn't," I observed.

"You might have," he countered, obviously feeling stronger now in his conviction.

"But what value does anything have if you can't say you got it right because you worked hard to earn the reward?"

I went on to explain that I myself certainly hadn't led a saint's life. I recalled the day when, at about age seven, I stole a candy bar from the corner drugstore. I told him I felt sick about it for days. I also confided that when I was taking tests in school, I occasionally thought about peeking over to the next desk for the right answer.

The urge to do so was sometimes so strong that I would have to put my hands up beside my face, like blinders.

McLean made it clear in that conversation that he didn't distinguish between being weak in the moment and being unable or unwilling to accept that some actions were by their very nature just plain wrong. I had let myself shrug off this problem with a simple promise to myself to talk with him at some later date about all this.

Because children arrive in the world without maintenance schedules, many of us often leave it to chance as we consider exactly when to make the necessary adjustments required for their safe passage through calamitous youth to reasonable adulthood. We do our tweaking at what seem like prudent intervals, maybe in reaction to a teacher's conference or upon hearing of transgressions made by the neighbors' kids. Or, like the weekend handyman, we might jump up and make a show of loud clanging and banging when the winds of change in our children's lives blow fierce out of the north and place in jeopardy peace on the home front.

I know I hadn't seen any marked signposts, hadn't discerned a precise moment when the planets were aligned just right to maximize the ability of my sons to grow in responsibility, kindness, and wisdom. All along

I'd been winging it, hedging my bets with a heavy dose of love and attention. And my sons responded to that nurturing by continually causing my chest to swell with pride and gratitude, lulling me into a false sense of security. Especially when I saw that their peers were taking on outsized importance and that the pressure to achieve threatened everywhere, I should have prepared for my sons a carefully conceived strategy to make it more than likely that the two would grow to be clear-thinking, honorable, caring, and successful adults. But I hadn't.

So, as I sat alone, spiritually sick over the reaction of my two sons to "Golf, the Great Game of Honor," I admonished myself to remember that talk alone is never enough. Somehow, some way, I needed to show Colin and McLean how honesty and integrity can be and should be made a central part of their lives. An effortless expression of these qualities needed to become habitual behavior. Before they could achieve that, though, they would have to be immersed in a world where right action felt like the norm.

And then I knew. Here it was, literally staring me in the face as the network returned to its coverage of golf. Golf *is* the game of honor. In what other sport is fair play revered with the same intensity as instances of outstanding performance?

INTRODUCTION

It was time for my sons and I to golf together, to experience the joys of the game together, time for me to explain the rules to them and inspire them to follow these rules with unyielding respect, whether playing alone on a summer's evening or in a tournament in front of thousands of people.

Personal integrity is on the run today. Rationalizations abound. I think we all know it, and I think we're all sad about it. We often experience our personal needs as so great that we insist on fulfilling them at any cost. But then the cost, it so often turns out, is the complete misery we feel in cowardice.

If I had anything to say about it, I thought as I regained my emotional equilibrium, my sons would not fall into this trap. I'd teach them how to acquire the courage of conviction, as we played as a family at a game I loved. We could, if my plan was sound, calibrate their moral compasses.

✳

I have just described the enterprise of teaching my sons to play golf as revealing itself to me in something like a moment of epiphany, suggesting a quite serious agenda. It was serious. But the tale I will tell you is of fathers and sons having fun. This is a chronicle of magical times.

It was magic I was seeking. I know we don't achieve a powerful bonding with our children without the intercession of grace. I was also aware, from personal experience, that the good fairies are fond of golf courses. And so I was confident that this plan to play golf with my sons offered us extraordinary possibilities.

As Colin and McLean grew from infants to little boys, and then threatened to become teenagers, I had been warned by friends and books that I should savor these various stages along the way. Conventional wisdom was that the early years with children are fleeting and uniquely wonderful times. There was the recurring suggestion that the clock is ticking, that the joys of parenthood are experienced as a game of diminishing returns. Ultimately, we were told, kids would come to think that hanging out with the parents is nothing but punishment.

I never placed much stock in this point of view, because my own experience of fatherhood was that it got better every step along the way. And yet, as Colin and McLean began to make it clear that the need to be among their peers was becoming the greatest need of all, I did fall prey to an apprehension that some day I wouldn't have them around enough to sufficiently satisfy my need for their closeness and camaraderie. So, I also viewed teaching them to play golf as a doorway into a new kind of relationship with them, a relationship that would be much more "adult." Up until that point, so much of our time together had been spent with me cheering and clapping while they played and performed on the hockey rink or soccer field. While I would always expect to be their biggest cheerleader, I knew the time had come for them to understand the importance of cheering a few of my shots along the way, as well.

In other words, I hoped that golf would become for us a lifelong method of coming together, of playing together, of appreciating life together. This is how it has been with my own father and myself. He loves the game of golf. Devoted to work and family, and a fellow who is most easily defined as provider, my father has always regarded golf as his refuge and his opportunity for play. Countless times, especially in his retirement years, he'd made it clear that playing golf with me and two of my brothers was his foretaste of the afterlife. For years, he'd planned and organized the "Shanley Tournament," in which he and I and Brian and Paul competed for family bragging rights and a little trophy he'd created. It was always one of the high points of my summer. I loved the thought of carrying the "Shanley Tournament" on into the next generation. I wanted to win the trophy at least forty more times.

Finally, I must confess that my greatest ambition of all in teaching my sons the game of golf was my intention to put them in touch with life's true flow, to enable them to understand what it meant to be at one with an experience.

For me, this is not an esoteric concept. In learning to play golf, I expected that my sons would come to appreciate the unmatchable beauty of experiencing the body, mind, and spirit working together. More important still, they would learn how to replicate this kind of experience, and in so doing, would discover what I believe is the very secret of life.

But it was the spiritual component of this adventure that made it tricky. I had little doubt that, in time, I could show my sons how body and mind working together could achieve a pleasurable or miserable union in the game of golf. I expected they would come to see how holding different thoughts in their heads produced different results in their ball-striking. If I accomplished this much alone, I would have provided them with an essential understanding of the game of life, as well as the game of golf.

But these are lessons derived from the relatively ordinary aspects of golf. What's extraordinary is the way the game simultaneously adheres to the principles of the mystical schools. It requires meditation, visualization, and total allegiance to the moment. It calls us to the higher laws, rewarding an inexhaustible eagerness to improve and humbling those who would be prideful. It takes us out under the sky, into the wind, where we either soar with the angels or get stuck in the sands of time. It allows us to appreciate sharing the joys and sorrows of our fellow players, as they cheer us or commiserate with us in our misfortunes. I have found no other place where men so willingly or easily submit themselves to these practices of faith, or demonstrate these finer virtues.

Children are inclined to believe that finding joy in life is as simple as satisfying their moment-to-moment needs. Unless we show them otherwise, they are likely to pursue this strategy of stringing together temporary satisfactions for the rest of their lives. I wanted my children to get past the temporal. I wished for them to have an altruistic, spiritual relationship with life, one that was marked by kindness and concern for others and not the exclusive pursuit of their own selfish needs. And while I didn't expect the game of golf to assume the entire burden of this goal, I knew it was well up to the task of helping me get them started on the path.

Everyone who has played golf with passion has had the experience of being "in the groove," for at least a few holes. With an almost unconscious ease, we strike the ball solidly, and it goes where we ask it to go. Judging the distance of our putts is automatic. We are one with the experience. There is no real separation between us and the swing and the ball in flight. We have lived the unity of body, mind, and spirit, and it is exhilarating.

In many sports, contestants often speak of reaching "the zone." Baseball players who have been "in the zone" describe being able to watch a 90-mile-an-hour fastball approach in slow motion, even being able to see the individual stitches on the ball. Basketball players say they sometimes know where a teammate will make a cut before he makes a move.

Golfers experience such ultimate excellence not as if they have taken a step out of time, or into some other world. Rather, we feel entirely present in the moment, with a heightened sense of touch and feel. We are in tune with the activity, to an extent often greater than at any other time in our lives. We feel in sync, we embrace a rhythm that feels completely natural to us, and it makes us crackle with energy and excitement.

INTRODUCTION

It is precisely this craving for being in the flow of the game that brings the avid golfer back to the course over and over, year after year. We can endure the agony of the slicing tee shot or wayward putting stroke because that one good stretch of holes, that one glorious round when it all comes together, tickles us in all our most ticklish spots. There we drink from the deepest well of life, and we are profoundly renewed.

It wasn't my intention to have my sons acquire a golfing addiction. If they did, fine. What I wanted for them, rather, was to grasp this concept of being in the groove, to be conscious of the power and majesty that are possible in the unity of body, mind, and spirit, and use this knowledge to make themselves good human beings.

Certainly they had been "in the groove" before, in other situations, riding their bikes through the woods or happily discovering right answers in the classroom. But they didn't know to make the most of these experiences, or to consider how and when to duplicate them. They hadn't yet learned how to appreciate what they had when they had it. They needed to be made aware that a conscious respect for being in the groove is absolutely critical to living a happy and fulfilling life.

Golf is a nearly perfect mechanism for learning to

recognize, value, and go with the flow of life. You can't muscle this game, nor can you con it. You simply can't do anything except remain humble while determined, at ease while focused, to have any hope at all of achieving success. You need to understand your emotions, to be unafraid of exploring their sources, and finally to make peace with them before moving on. And, of course, so it is with life.

And so it is with the making of good relationships between fathers and sons.

This book is really about the love between fathers and sons, an often difficult love. Men are shy at the door-step of their emotional and spiritual selves, and are in-clined to step back from them, retreating to more familiar territory. Sons often learn from mimicking just this er-ratic behavior of their fathers.

The love between fathers and sons is also full of promise. There's no joy like finally coming to peace with a difficult relationship.

✢

When I told Colin and McLean that I wanted to get them started playing golf, they were both enthusiastic. They were also a little apprehensive, because they were perceptive enough to see the weight I was placing on this enterprise. But I've played all of my very best rounds of golf feeling very eager and at least a little nervous, so as we began our adventure early that summer I had great faith in our prospects.

What follows is an account of that summer and fall when I taught my sons to play golf—and learned a tremendous amount about them and me and a grand old game.

When you hit a poor shot and find yourself in trouble, train yourself never to become truly upset. Maybe you've played ten or twelve holes very well to this point. There's no reason to let one bad shot ruin a good round. Even if you aren't having an extra good day, you should always count your blessings. Be thankful that you are able to be out on a beautiful course playing. Many people in the world don't have that opportunity, for one reason or another.

—FRED COUPLES

✽

1

*

BEGINNING WITH APPRECIATION

I needed to keep the innocent out of the crossfire.

Struggling for nonchalance, I asked the clean-cut young golf shop salesman in the pressed khaki pants and pale blue golf shirt if he would mind giving my sons and me a minute alone. Shrugging his shoulders, the youth walked off, disappearing among the rows of brightly colored golf bags. He had probably witnessed his share of family feuding in the shop, I considered as I watched him go, or maybe he was just unflappable.

Colin, McLean, and I had already spent a good quarter hour examining various sets of clubs in this little shop. While I had previously stopped in here a few times to use the driving range that was part of the facility, I had paid little attention to all the golfing equipment that filled the rather cramped space. They stocked every brand name of club I'd ever heard of, and just as many more that I had not. The bags—fat, thin, and in between— came in a full spectrum of colors. Facing this selection, I felt overwhelmed. The boys, on the other hand, had at once begun pulling clubs from the display racks, attempting swings with little regard for the damage they might cause, never mind the bodily harm they might inflict on the shop's other patrons. I had needed to take each of them by the arm, advising them that if they did not control themselves, we would be leaving at once. Only slightly less exuberant, they had proceeded then to touch or point out every object in sight as an object of their affection, before I finally won the attention of the salesman and he narrowed our search to clubs and bags suitable for young beginners.

Taking a deep breath, I refocused my attention on Colin, who remained defiant, continuing to hold fast to the driver from an expensive golf set that I had already rejected twice.

"Look," I said, "this is the last time I'm going to say this, and then you walk out of here empty-handed. You're not getting that set of clubs." I folded my arms in front of me as decisively as possible as I continued to stare him down.

Colin was short for his age, as I had been. But while the lack of stature had tended to keep my will in check, it had served to strengthen his. My earliest memories of him were his barreling down hilly driveways on his brightly colored plastic three-wheeler, leaning forward to accelerate, his little teeth gritted and bared. Whenever he cried, which was rare, we knew he was really hurt, because he never used tears for mere sympathy. Whenever he worked on a project—say, fashioning a boomerang from plywood with just the right angle to make it really work—he wouldn't stop to talk or eat or sleep until he was satisfied with the final product. When I got him started playing hockey at age six, he was as energetic as a little bee buzzing in and out among the bigger boys. At practice, he seemed to relish the drills, always trying to be the first to get up and down the ice, his short legs pumping twice as hard. Despite his willfullness, he was very coachable. I'd make a suggestion that he might try taking the puck to the left, because a defenseman could predict where he was going, and on the very next play I would see him test out the idea, satisfying himself that it really made sense.

There's little of this ferocity in Colin's outward appearance. He has full, round cheeks and soft skin. Thick brown hair flops down easily across his forehead over soft gray-green eyes. Below the neck, the picture is a little more indicative: There isn't an ounce of fat on him; he's all tensile strength.

"I'll pay the difference," Colin insisted. "If I'm willing to work and pay the difference in cost, I don't see what the problem is. These are the golf clubs I want."

I inhaled slowly through my nose, then exhaled noisily again, hoping he'd begin to appreciate the depth of my displeasure. Sure, money was an issue. They hadn't even played their first round, yet I was spending $200 in order to get them both a new bag and a new junior set comprised of a driver and putter and five-, seven-, and nine-iron.

I'd given the subject considerable thought, because I do believe that the right clubs do make a difference. That difference doesn't warrant the hysteria that surrounds the new golf club technologies, for too many people now tend to blame the club when they should work on their swing. However, five years earlier, when my father had handed down a set of excellent irons and I finally gave up the clubs I'd used since high school, I saw the immediate difference they made in my iron play. And, despite how much I miss the feel of a wooden club well struck, I know my metals are far more forgiving of an imperfect swing.

BEGINNING WITH APPRECIATION

Initially, I'd planned to find old sets of ladies' clubs and have them cut down to size for the boys, but I soon realized that a set of junior clubs would be more suitably weighted. With them Colin and McLean would stand a better chance of hitting good shots, and hitting good shots early on would be critical to sustaining their morale.

Yet, I couldn't help but think back to when I was their age. I started out choking down on the overly long, ancient clubs my father had left neglected among the cobwebs in the back corner of the garage. My brother Michael and I played with whiffle balls and carved out a course around the back and side yards, using trees as targets. When I finally got my first set of junior clubs I felt as if I'd hit the lottery.

I'd also read how Seve Ballesteros, considered one of the truly great players in the history of the game, never had his own set of new clubs until he turned professional at age sixteen. He'd had to beg members to let him borrow their clubs in order to play in caddie championships.

"Colin," I said sternly, "if you can't be appreciative, you'll never be able to love the game of golf. You may get so you appear to be a good player, but you won't be happy playing. Lack of appreciation for a nice walk on a summer's day or lack of appreciation for a couple of well-played holes turns the game into torture."

Colin crinkled up the left side of his face, clearly nonplussed by the direction my argument was taking. While I wasn't well prepared for this particular conversation, I had intended to make this point with my sons early on in our golfing summer.

"Golf, at least as I am going to teach it to you and your brother, is a game that will expose all of your weaknesses as well as your strengths," I explained. "It won't let you get away with anything. Try to take a shortcut, and you usually get murdered. Try to play golf in some half-baked way, and you'll never be very good. You see, if you don't appreciate golf, it doesn't appreciate you either."

Colin was looking around him, checking to see if anyone besides his brother, who stood nearby, was listening in on our conversation. "Dad, you're being a little weird aren't you?" he said. "Golf's only a game, and I'm only talking about getting different clubs."

I smiled. "I know that's all *you're* talking about," I replied. "I'm talking about something much bigger and more important. Appreciation."

Colin closed his eyes for a long moment. He clearly didn't want to have this discussion, which we were both all too well aware threatened to ignite the embers that had long been smoldering between us. For the past month he'd been spending all of his odd-jobs money on expensive accessories for his mountain bike, in a mad dash to keep up with his friends. I hadn't stopped him, but I'd repeatedly called him on it, reminding him that he hardly seemed to appreciate the new tires or the new seat before he needed something else.

"I'm spending a hundred dollars on you here this morning," I continued. "We don't even know if you'll like playing golf. And yet, all I've heard out of you is a complaint. Don't you think that's pretty outrageous?"

It was barely perceptible, but I saw Colin wince. Only weeks before, this would have been enough to make me back off. I'd never been able to hammer him without feeling like I'd violated a silent but sacred pact between us: If I'd give him the freedom to be himself, he would reveal regions of my soul where I had never traveled.

When Colin was born and first placed in my arms, the overwhelming impression I had of him was that he was entirely his own person. If I had cherished some grand notion that my first child would represent an extension of my family tree, that we would be alike in so many ways, this idea was immediately obliterated. I was overwhelmed by the awareness that he had his very own life, his own destiny, and would take up his own space in the world.

This recognition had, at first, startled me. Had I really never considered that my children would be individuals? Had my need for closeness so overwhelmed me? Yes, and yes. But moving past the initial shock, I soon discovered that Colin and I would nonetheless extend each other unconditional love, feeling it most powerfully as we noticed how differently we sometimes experienced our lives, together and alone. I found this all quite thrilling.

Colin and I had already been through a lot together. His mother and I divorced when he was nine. The day we told him, he got up into my arms and wept openly, imploring me not to go. That I was only moving a couple of miles across town and would see him nearly every day mattered to him not at all. It was the most devastating experience of my life. But in the months that followed he was brave and open in conversation with me about how deeply the separation of his parents affected him. I'll never forget the evening that this little boy, eyes glistening, said that while he hated that his mother and I would not always be together, he wanted me to be happy and he knew that I would never purposely do anything to cause him pain.

But here in the golf shop as we stood facing each other off, there was nothing cosmic at work, and I knew it. Plainly and simply stated, here was a thirteen-year-old boy who was being a little brat.

"Colin," I said, forging ahead, trying to explain. "You're going to miss a lot of shots when you start playing golf, and if you miss a few and decide the whole game stinks, then your whole game really will start to stink. Golf is like that. Believe me, I know."

I paused. While I knew it was good fortune that I was able to introduce this lesson so early on, it would need to be integrated into and reinforced in nearly every golfing lesson. It would only be learned over time. Truth be told, I had finally learned it myself just recently, and it had taken a trip all the way across the ocean to do so.

When Karen and I were married two years before, we went to Ireland for our honeymoon. We had no planned itinerary, other than to arrive at Shannon Airport, rent a car, and see the country. The first day, in search of the Cliffs of Moher, designated on the map as one of those places we shouldn't miss, we quite serendipitously discovered the charming little seaside town of Lahinch, and the renowned Lahinch Golf Club. The course was designed by "Old" Tom Morris of St. Andrews, who reportedly said upon its completion in 1893,

"I consider the links as fine a natural course as it has ever been my good fortune to play over."

Because Karen's not a golfer, I had not brought my clubs along. We both knew that I might find a way to play, but neither of us would worry if it didn't manage to happen. But winding up on the very first day of our trip in a town with a legendary golf course made it happen fast. And the golfing experience we would share there was to set the tone for what would prove to be the best honeymoon a pair of newlyweds could ever hope to have.

I called over to the Lahinch pro shop around six that evening and explained to the pro that I had no clubs and no reservation, but wondered if I might find a way to play the old course early that next morning before we set off to see the rest of Ireland. He hesitated only long enough to check the roster.

"There'll be a members tournament in the morning," he said. "But if you'll be here at seven A.M., you can get off before it begins. I'll leave you a set of clubs inside the back door. It will be open. And will you be needing balls?"

I could hardly speak. He'd be leaving the door open? Did I need balls? "Oh, yes," I stammered, "I'll need balls. Thanks. Thanks very much."

"I'll put two sleeves in the bag," he said. "That's seven A.M. sharp. Don't be late."

I put the phone down slowly and turned to face my bride. "He's going to leave the door open for me, and he's going to leave me balls in the bag. We didn't just cross a time zone getting here, we slipped into a parallel universe."

We had indeed. This matter-of-fact kindness and native good will was to follow us everywhere we went over the next nine days.

"Did I hear you say seven A.M.?" Karen asked. She had previously offered, gracious as ever, to walk the course with me.

"I've got to get off before a members tournament," I apologized. "You don't have to come if you don't want. I'll be quick. I'll be back here at the hotel by ten."

I studied her expression carefully, searching for any sign at all that I had hurt her feelings, trespassed on her honeymoon dreams.

At thirty-eight, Karen retained her girlish good looks. In the damp Irish air her thick blonde hair looked ready to rebel at any moment, to curl up into tight little ringlets, to throw off the yoke of the day's steady, hard brushing. She hadn't a single wrinkle on her face, and her green eyes were bright and clear. It hadn't occurred to her for a moment that at her relatively advanced age she should temper her expectations for our honeymoon. I had made the terrible mistake several months earlier of admitting that, since this was my second marriage, I found it a little hard to get all worked up over wedding preparations. Though she quickly hid it, her obvious hurt had been stern rebuke to my selfishness. I wasn't going to let it happen again.

She met my gaze evenly. "We're married now," she said. "We do things together."

So it was together that we walked the links at La-hinch, and what a wonderful walk it was.

We arrived at the course at 6:50 A.M. The side door to the pro shop was open as promised, and two sleeves of brand-new balls had been slipped into the bag. I noted with pleasure that the set included an old wooden driver and three-wood. What better way to play the old course, than with *real* woods?

As we strolled onto the course the wind was whipping sharply off the ocean, and I noticed that the pin on the first green was bent over at a forty-five-degree angle. It was also starting to rain. But I was raring to go. From the pro shop I had seen that this golf course was like no other I had previously encountered. There wasn't a single tree across the entire landscape, just pastureland and enormous dunes.

I lost four balls in the first two holes before I got with the program and began teeing the ball down low, still allowing for huge carries with the wind. I made very sure that I did everything I could to stay out of the rough, because this was rough worthy of its name: Barely five feet off the fairway, the grass had grown to a height above my knees.

Karen laughed a lot at my performance. On the fifth, the wind blew my ball from the tee three times before I had a chance to strike it. On the sixth, called the Dell, one of the most famous holes in Irish golf, the par-three's green is nestled between two steep sand dunes and completely blind from the tee. Only a white stone on the face of the front hill indicates where the pin is located.

It wasn't until the back nine that I finally began to get the hang of Irish golf, putting together a string of pars and bogeys. By then, Karen was much less interested in my game than finding the goats that wander the links, and watching the seagulls that flew dead still for seconds at a time as they tried to fly against the wind, before finally being swooped away by it, instantly achieving the speed of jet fighter pilots. Playing with the wind, I hit a three-wood to the green of a 244-yard par four. Against the wind, I hit a good drive, solid three-wood, and then a full five-iron to a 418-yard par four.

Before driving rain finally chased us away after fifteen holes, we met an old Irish fellow who seemed to be wandering the course with no real purpose, though he may have been a ranger. "Nice day," he said as we approached him. "Bit of a breeze."

I waited for his smile. Had there really been no hint of irony in his voice? It was impossible even to stand up straight. As we watched the fellow move off as quickly as he had appeared, Karen and I looked at each other.

"Bit of a breeze," I said.

"Bit of a breeze," she agreed, and we laughed.

It was the most wondrous morning of golf I'd ever experienced—entirely unexpected, rich with sights and sounds and smells, born of kindness, demanding my complete attention, and shared with someone I loved. It made me completely happy.

When the next summer came around, I couldn't wait to play golf. The round at Lahinch had left an indelible impression, and I played the game that season with greater skill than I ever had before.

✳

Awakening from my daydream, I turned my attention to Colin.

"I'd say you've blown it here this morning," I told him. "That's really all there is to it. You should be happy just to have the opportunity to play the game, to have any clubs at all."

"I am appreciative," he said evenly. "I just like the other clubs more."

I scanned the shop for the young man who had been helping us, and when I looked back, Colin was still holding the fancy driver with the multicolored shaft.

"I'm going to save my own money and buy this other set," he said defiantly.

I shook my head, but my anger and frustration were spent. What I chose to hear now in his stubbornness was that he planned on sticking with golf. He was talking about his future in the game.

"I'll tell you what," I said, realizing it was time to compromise. "When you break one hundred, I'll buy you an entire set, with all the woods and irons."

Colin hesitated, then smiled.

"Me too, Dad?" McLean chimed in. Apparently he'd decided it was safe now to be seen and heard from again.

McLean had inherited my long, angular face, blue eyes, and fine dirty-blond hair. He, too, was lean and moved with an easy, shuffling gate. But whereas his physical makeup closely matched mine, his emotional makeup did not. It was often difficult to know what McLean was thinking or feeling, for he kept his emotions carefully guarded. It was more than a sensitive boy's shyness; he rarely cried, and his most overt display of happiness was a sort of three-quarter smile. He'd pinch that last quarter, holding it in reserve as if he feared he'd lose consciousness if he surrendered to the emotion. He just wasn't going to let himself go too far—not with anything. He quickly accepted limitations, embracing them for their familiar comfort. Currently, he defined himself as an ace student and star soccer player. He excelled in these two areas, and that was enough. In every other area of life he showed an often annoying carelessness and inattention. I felt I needed to start him on the process of understanding that everything matters. He needed help in mining the depths of his feelings, and expressing them once he found them.

"You too, McLean," I said. "But neither of you should underestimate how tough it will be to break one hundred. Many, many people never get there."

"Maybe a month," Colin said, never one to resist a challenge.

"Maybe a few weeks," McLean said, ever vigilant in his effort not to let his older brother get the upper hand.

My emotional equilibrium restored, we purchased the two junior sets and two bags, along with a half-dozen golf balls.

We were nearly to the car when Colin stopped. He pulled the driver from his new bag and stepped over to a grassy area near the parking lot. He took a few swings.

"Feels pretty good," he announced as he hitched the bag over his shoulder and swaggered toward us.

I nodded.

"Come on," I said. "Let's go see what happens when we put a golf ball down in front of you."

I don't try to teach golf to children. What they need is someone who will guide their learning. Let them play, then help them when they want you to, or when you see something that demands a teacher's attention.

—HARVEY PENICK

✷

2

*

SWINGING AWAY

If ever there was a place to enjoy the game of golf without the cost of membership in a private club, it's Saratoga Springs, New York. We live in a restored 1830s farmhouse, just across the town line, where it turns to countryside, but Murphy's driving range, the oldest driving range and miniature golf center in the country, is just three miles from our front door. Across the road from the range, down the stately Avenue of the Pines, is the Saratoga Spa State Park, with its eighteen-hole course and nine-hole, par-three layout. During July and August, when Saratoga Race Course, the oldest Thoroughbred race track in the country, attracts horsemen, socialites, gamblers, and horseracing fans from around the country, the state park attracts legions of golfers. But on many evenings from May to October one can play an entire round with hardly a wait.

Of course, the boys would have had us on the first tee of the eighteen-hole course as fast as we could get back to town with their new clubs, but they had no illusions about where we would be heading first. I had been telling them over and over for days that we would have to spend hours at the driving range before we actually played. I had already repeated the mantra that would be intoned ad infinitum in the weeks and months ahead: *The swing has to be grooved. The swing is everything.*

I have never had a formal golf lesson, but I caddied every summer from ages twelve to seventeen at Warwick Country Club in Warwick, Rhode Island. Donald Ross, the Scotsman who designed many of New England's most interesting and challenging golf courses, created this layout that occupies the end of a peninsula reaching out into Narragansett Bay. It was about a fifteen-minute drive from my parents' home, usually a half-hour hitchhike at 7 A.M. for a young boy in shorts, sneakers, and a golf shirt.

Caddying is the best program of lessons in golf anybody could have. As caddies, we became masters at imitation. Before Peter Jacobsen began doing imitations of his fellow golfing professionals, we were behind the caddy shack mimicking the swings of the members. I modeled my swing after that of Tim Harrington, who was close to a scratch player during those years in the mid- to late sixties. He drew his club back in a wide, sweeping motion, something like Davis Love III does today, and followed through way up high. All these years later, I still think of him whenever my swing needs work.

Since my father was a club member, in addition to playing on "Caddy's Day," which was Monday, I was on the course on "Junior Golf Day," which was Tuesday, and then I played or practiced almost every afternoon after I finished caddying. In other words, I had plenty of opportunity to groove my own swing as a young player.

I was more than a little anxious as I anticipated helping Colin and McLean develop their swings, because I had come to believe that the swings we have at our beginnings as golfers remain with us for life.

This perception had first struck me the previous summer. In the first round of a member-guest tournament I played in with my father at his club, one of our opponents was a fellow who'd played junior golf with me. In fact, he'd once beaten me in the semifinals of the junior club championship and sent me into days of depression. On the second hole of the match we were now engaged in, nearly thirty years since he'd dashed my championship dreams, he drew up alongside me after I'd hit my tee shot. "Your swing hasn't changed a bit," he said smiling wryly.

This innocent comment put me momentarily into shock. His observation didn't seem possible. When I was playing golf as a young teenager, I probably didn't stand much more than five feet four inches tall, and weighed no more than 110 pounds. I'd grown to become a five-foot ten-and-a-half-inch, 165-pound man. I could hit the ball much farther. In the weeks before this tournament I had spent hours at the driving range modifying my swing pattern . . . and then I realized that I had been thinking the same thing as I watched him swing: Someone could have put a bag over his head on the first tee, and I would have known who it was.

This notion of the signature swing's being developed very early on was further reinforced by a cover article I had read in *Golf* magazine that winter which concluded that, for better and worse, the swing we demonstrate after just our first few rounds is pretty much the swing we're stuck with. We can tinker with it here and there, but these adjustments will be barely visible to the naked eye. To buttress their argument, the writers of the article asked us to consider the big-name golfers who have pro-claimed that they have achieved major makeovers of their swings. They argued, in effect, that you could take the young Jack Nicklaus (before he'd "changed" his swing a hundred times) and put him in a clever disguise, but his swing would give him away in a second to anybody who has seen him play today as one of the game's most distinguished senior citizens.

✻

When we arrived at Murphy's driving range that first afternoon after we'd bought the boys their new clubs, my plan was to give Colin and McLean a brief exhibition. They would watch as I struck a few irons and then attempt to replicate my swing. I'd been told often over the years that I have a pretty good swing, so I hoped—actually, expected—that my sons would be eager to imitate me.

In fact, the boys had no interest whatsoever in watching their old man hit, though I am embarrassed to admit that it took me several long minutes before I realized as much. I'd gotten off five or six shots, instructing all the while about what they should be noticing about my body, hands, arms, and head, before I came up for air. As soon as I looked at them, I knew.

They just wanted to hit.

Of course. Before anything else could happen, they

needed to have their own direct experience with the game. They needed to develop their own relationship with golf. They would never pay much attention to me, and they would never pay much attention to golf, unless they truly thought the game mattered. The only way the game could matter was if it brought them joy and satisfaction, if it promised them reward for their efforts. At the moment, all they had was my word for it that this would be the case.

Even the world's greatest teachers, in whatever discipline, can make little headway against indifference. I'd heard it said time and again: You can't give anyone your experience. You can only create an opportunity for a person to have his own experience. You can't give anyone your feeling for something, no matter how captivating you may be, no matter how much feeling you may be generating on your own.

I certainly knew this, but I was so consumed by my desire to share, and my relationship with golf seemed to impart so much insight, that I had been momentarily knocked off kilter.

My on-again, off-again romance with golf coincided with some of the more dramatic ebbs and flows of my existence. When I was twelve my family moved, and I didn't handle the dislocation well. We had relocated only five miles across town, but it seemed like five thousand miles, because the old neighborhood and all my pals were all I'd known or wanted to know. My parents tried to push me and my brother Michael out of the house to meet the local kids, but it was months before we made new friends. The loneliness was a terrible ache.

It wasn't too long afterward that my father joined Warwick Country Club and I began to caddy and play golf. From the start, I loved the job and I loved the game. It was here that I first earned money of my own, here that I learned about the facts of life, learned to play blackjack and poker for money, learned to enjoy myself, and learned to play golf, eventually well enough to break 80. I thought nothing of caddying eighteen holes and then playing eighteen or twenty-seven holes until there was no light left in the day. We competed in putting tournaments on the putting green that held all the tension and drama of the Masters. I passed many, many days as youth should be privileged to experience them, as served up to me for the sole purpose of extracting as much pleasure from them as possible.

When I got to college, I tried out for the golf team and, because on both qualifying days I ended my rounds with disastrous finishes, I did not make the starting five. Within one short season, I dropped away from the team and did not pick up a club for the next ten years. I grew my hair long and marched through college with a bad attitude and a feeling that life held no purpose for me. Eventually, I would marry, have children, and do a decade-long stint as a newspaper reporter, but I was still plagued by the knowledge that I couldn't quite find my way. I couldn't sustain a smile, or an eagerness to take the relentless challenges of existence.

In my late thirties, I found myself writing copy for an advertising agency. Like many in my generation, difficult economic circumstances and profound fatigue at tilting at windmills had finally forced me to make choices based on what might earn me a decent living. And there I was, thrown in with some colleagues who liked playing golf. So, as I began righting myself in the effort to become a productive citizen, I began to play golf again. Over the next decade, a period that was not without its own turmoil and change, I put together a very solid life and I brought my golf game back as well. By my early forties, I was married for the second time to a most extraordinary woman, and was shooting in the seventies. *I'm back*, I would say to myself with a sense of joy and relief, for which I was profoundly grateful.

Golf and I had formed our own special relationship,

very much determined by my circumstances and by my personal needs as they developed along the way. My sons would need to find golf as they chose to find it. Maybe they'd love it and maybe they wouldn't. Maybe they'd want to master it, and maybe they would treat it casually.

The lessons that genuinely matter are learned in the doing. My sons would have no desire to heed my teaching until they had taken their own swings and determined that maybe their swings might be in need of some modification and that, in improving them, their desires or ambitions might be better served. First, they needed to determine if they really liked golf, to see if it produced a sense of wonder as well as accomplishment. First, they needed to find their own swings without the distractions of advice about balance and grace and following through. They had no reason to view golf as the grand metaphor for the making of their lives; they just wanted to smack that ball and see how far they could send it flying.

Realizing this, I threw my club against my bag, divided the bucket of balls in two, showed each one of them how to form a grip, and encouraged them to swing away.

Actually, they did quite well. Scattered among all the tops and duffs, and despite the irreverence of their comments about "jamming on it," and the shameless braggadocio that followed anything resembling solid contact, there were shots that flew straight and true.

Later, I would receive confirmation of my instinct to let my sons find their own swings while reading Fred Couples's book, *Total Shotmaking*. Couples believes he's been successful in golf because he taught himself. That big, loose swing is entirely his creation, he says, and it just feels right, and always has. What's so critical about having a swing that his body wants to make, he argues, is that it can be repeated consistently—even under championship pressure.

As golf has become more and more popular in recent years, many have learned to play as adults, when the body is not as loose, and its motions less fluid. Lessons are probably in order right away for a middle-aged fellow who may have lost a few steps since the high school football days.

But kids can learn as naturals, thriving on cheers. So, as I stood back to let Colin and McLean swing away, I assumed the role of cheerleader. This is a critical role in golfing instruction, since for anyone learning the game, the missed shots always far outweigh those well struck. As the hours passed I found so many ways to put a happy face on a horrid shot that I figured I'd earned the right to try out for the position of Presidential Press Secretary.

I did not remain entirely a spectator, however. There are those habits that can become much too difficult to break, and I just couldn't take the risk that the boys would fall into them. I knew they would be forever thankful if they learned from the start to sweep the club back with the left arm straight, making the backswing a careful, considered motion.

"Sweep it back and sweep it through," I said at intervals. "Hackers chop at the ball. No hackers in this family. Sweep it back and sweep it through."

As difficult as it was not to meddle more, I mostly let them have their fun.

It was inevitable that almost immediately they both began trying to hit the ball as hard and far as they could. I would soon have to work on getting them to develop an easy tempo to their swings, but not in this initial session.

I remember how as a kid, long before I actually played golf, I would bounce golf balls on the street and watch them shoot up as high as the tops of telephone poles. With a couple of friends, I journeyed by bike one Saturday morning into town to the Little League baseball field, where we smacked golf balls with baseball bats, knocking them way out of the park with ease, a feat I had never been able to accomplish in my otherwise stellar Little League career.

In golf it's not easy to hit a ball well when you're trying to poke it over the fence, my sons learned. After they calmed down a bit, they both showed a willingness to concentrate. They also demonstrated an ability to make a good swing. That didn't really surprise me, since both were good athletes. But I was surprised that Colin had the more controlled swing. He spread his feet somewhat wide and kept his backswing short. There wasn't enough flex in the knees, and he had a tendency to go back on his heels, but he was quickly finding a way to achieve consistently solid contact. McLean, meanwhile, was allowing his backswing to get the better of him. He was making a rather graceful, looping arch with the club, but he was letting his hands go up so high that he was often leaving himself a downswing barreling out of control.

I had expected the complete reverse in their swing patterns. Colin skis steep mountain slopes with reckless abandon, jumping moguls, seeking out trails through the trees. Bored by inactivity, he is ever searching for that next exciting experience. Actually, I had worried, and I think he had too, that he might find golf boring.

McLean, on the other hand, thrives on routine, needs to sit at the same place at the table every night or the food doesn't taste right. And he simply can't be rushed. Whenever it was time to go anywhere, it seemed, Colin and I would be standing at the door, while McLean made a project of tying the laces on his shoes. I had him pegged as my golfing protégé; he would be temperamentally well suited to the game's easy rhythms.

And yet here was Colin hitting two out of five balls with pretty good contact, while carefully monitoring his own body movements. A few paces away, his younger brother did his John Daly swing, crashing one, missing the next completely, apparently unconcerned about making any adjustments.

I couldn't help but smile throughout this exhibition, not just because I had been shown up to be a completely unreliable prognosticator, but also because both my sons were so clearly having a great time. When all the balls from the large bucket had been hit, they begged me to buy them each their own.

I bought two more large buckets, and would have bought them another, glad as I was that golf had my sons in its clutches and wouldn't let them loose, but I'd run out of money.

"Enough for today," I said. "There's a full summer ahead."

✲

That evening, Karen and I were sitting out on the back deck in the glider, swaying back and forth, sharing a wool blanket stretched across our knees.

"So, it sounds like the golf part went well today," Karen said. I'd filled her in on the incident at the golf shop, but hadn't said much about our experience at the driving range.

"Yes, all in all, I think it really did," I said, and then hesitated. "But you know," I continued, "I got way off in my head today, watching the two of them hitting the ball. I kept wondering, *Why golf?* Why did I love it so much right from the beginning? Did I come to it by default?"

"What started all that?" Karen asked. "Did something else happen?"

We continued our silent swaying as I pondered her question. I noticed that our cat, a small gray tiger we'd rescued from the pound the previous summer to rid the house of its mice, was crouched low at the base of the locust tree to my left. Lilly had not only scared the mice from the house, she'd been stripping the property of baby rabbits, birds, and anything else with the temerity to trespass within her kingdom. I appreciated that she was such an able hunter, and that she was so thoroughly wild, and didn't have to agonize over why she was put on the planet or how she should spend her days and nights. She was either asleep, or entirely focused on the hunt. The total lack of angst in her life was envious. But when she would bring her prey into the house for the final killing ritual, I found it hard to like her. Even Karen, whose fondness for animals was far greater than mine, talked of taking her back to the pound. But of course we never would. She was part of the menagerie, having been befriended by Kiera. Kiera was Karen's Shetland sheepdog, and theirs was a relationship predating ours. From the beginning it had been made clear to me that Kiera had been Karen's first love and thus would always command exalted status. Kiera extended me the benefit of the doubt, while I continued to begrudge her position on high. She was seated now off to Karen's right, the lion guarding her queen.

"No, nothing happened," I said. "I was just surprised by how Colin really tried hard to figure out how to hit the ball consistently well. McLean was just blasting away.

You should have seen him," I said, chuckling. "He was a wild man. He tried hitting every one out of the park . . ."

Karen waited, and seeing me lost in thought, finally asked, "So how did that get you thinking about why you love golf?"

"Oh, I don't know," I answered, sighing. "I was standing there watching McLean and I just got off on this thing about whether he and I were really that much alike. . . . You know how everybody says we look so much alike, the way Colin looks like a carbon copy of his mother. And McLean and I both tend to be homebodies, both of us are happy just to hang out, both of us like singing along to rock and roll.

"I was thinking that maybe I've been reading too much into this. How much *are* McLean and I really alike?"

"What did you decide?" Karen asked, when I wasn't immediately forthcoming.

I hadn't decided. I just knew that when I was McLean's age and in love with baseball, I spent hours throwing a ball against the side of the house, learning to catch the caroms. When I took up golf, I accumulated dozens of old balls for my own practice bag and went trudging out to the far corner of Warwick Country Club where we were allowed to hit them. McLean hadn't shown me that there was anything he wanted badly enough to really go for it.

Colin's experience with sports was much more like mine. I was a star in neighborhood games, but couldn't pass muster at the varsity level. I showed up for the first day of high school football practice and was Gulliver in the land of the giants. I ran away from there as fast as a ninety-nine-pound weakling could run.

It was the same thing with baseball. I got picked for the all-star team every year in Little League, but in the Babe Ruth league these big guys were throwing hard curveballs. I kept stepping back before swinging. If I made contact, it was with the end of the bat. The ball would go spinning weakly down the first-base line. It was humiliating . . . I wasn't good enough to make the high school golf team either. I finally settled for tennis because hardly anybody tried out for the tennis team in those days. Tennis was for sissies.

I knew Karen had a hard time understanding all this. She'd never cared about any of this. Not even remotely. She'd had her circle of close friends in high school, and that was all that mattered. She played field hockey for "fun," but basically thought organized sports were highly overrated.

My lessons in humility weren't limited to sports. It was the same thing with school. In elementary school I was the proverbial big fish in a small pond. A's without working up a sweat, a wizard at dodgeball, the whole package. Then I got to junior high and bang, I got three C's in the first marking period.

Overall, I did pretty well in high school. I had a lot of friends, and was active in school politics. But I never felt like I measured up. I doubted my ability to achieve the lofty goals I'd always had for my life. The older I got, the more I second-guessed myself. Members of my family continued to hear all the brave talk about how one day I'd be rich and famous, but for the life of me I didn't know how I'd ever distinguish myself. Sometimes the fear of failure was energizing. Other times I retreated to my bedroom and sulked.

"I just don't want my kids to spend as much time as I did getting down on themselves," I said, looking back over at Karen. "I wish there was some way that they could learn from my mistakes."

"Maybe they will," Karen said. "You're doing all you can to share your life with them. What they do with it is starting to become their responsibility now. They aren't your little babies anymore."

We were silent. The crickets, on the other hand,

played with a full orchestra in the swampy woods across the lawn from us. I found it astonishing how much noise they could generate.

"So, did you ever figure out why you love golf?" Karen asked after some time had passed.

"I don't think I did," I said. "I got caught up in thinking that I got to golf because I'd flunked out of everything else, and golf was just my way of staying in the competitive arena. I've always needed to compete."

"I hate to disappoint you dear, but I don't think you're as competitive as you think you are," Karen said.

I looked over at her and frowned. "Yeah, right," I said.

I turned back to face the woods. The treetops were in dark silhouette against a charcoal sky. Not competitive? That was a misperception. I'd played every game I ever played to win. My father said I sometimes cried when my Little League team lost.

"What I mean is that you don't really enjoy competing against other people," Karen said, finally offering a clarification. "The competition you like is against yourself. That's why you ran those ridiculous marathons. You love beating yourself."

I wasn't so sure. Maybe I didn't take much joy in getting the better of others, but I sure loved proving to other people that I was good. The best way was usually to beat them. Was there a difference here?

"I avoid conflict," I said. "But I certainly enjoy beating people at games."

"That's because beating them seems to provide you with the best yardstick of success," Karen said. "That's what you learned as a boy. That's what all little boys learn. But I think one of the reasons you like golf is because you can play against the golf course. Beating somebody else in a match is secondary, or at least that's how you talk about it."

"That's true," I said. "That really is true."

"So golf gives you all the excitement of sport, which you seem to crave," Karen said, "without creating the enemies."

I looked at her and smiled. "It's just not easy being a guy."

"Not anything I ever cared to be," she replied.

Of this I had no doubt. Karen could be forceful, and was never one to be trifled with, but she was definitely a girl. She liked pretty things in delicate patterns. She enjoyed whispering secrets and terms of endearment. Her most ardently held dream was that we would live to spend our days together in the garden wearing His and Her floppy hats.

Karen was willing to take up golf so that we could play together, but I wasn't encouraging. We'd tried that briefly one night the previous summer. She'd whacked at the ball like Alice with her live flamingo at the Queen's croquet game: missing, missing again, laughing, moving the ball ten feet to the left, laughing some more. I'd begged her to stop, and thankfully she had, content to walk along beside me as I played my much more serious game.

Maybe it was because golf was my own first true love, my first solid connection with a feeling of joy. I knew golf wasn't going to win me the approval of my peers or make me popular. There wouldn't be people standing on the sidelines cheering. There was none of that pressure, none of those needs. It was a pure joy I felt. And I felt it as much when by myself on a summer's night as I did playing in tournaments.

"Being a guy does have its privileges," I said.

"Oh, and what might they be?" Karen asked.

"Sometimes the guy gets the girl," I said.

"You're sweet," she said.

"I'm learning," I replied.

✼

In the first week after we bought the clubs and got them started, the boys, to my delight, pestered me repeatedly about getting out again to the range. They'd been using their nine-irons on the side lawn, often taking up nasty divots, but getting the feel for the pitch shot.

It seemed that they were showing sufficient interest in the game that I could now feel free to introduce a little classtime into the mix. This was a misjudgment on my part.

When I came home from the library one night that first week with a Jack Nicklaus instructional video, you'd have thought I'd announced that summer vacation had been suspended. I hadn't expected them to greet this tape with the same fervor they might a movie in which buildings were blown up and cars sent careening wildly around city streets, but I was taken aback by their hostility to the very idea of it.

My first impulse was to chastise. Did they think themselves so naturally gifted that they couldn't benefit from instruction by the greatest player of the past four decades?

But then I stopped myself in time to consider the experience my sons had had with sports up to that point in their lives.

It's a sad fact that children rarely seem to organize their own games anymore. They don't simply troop off together to the back lot, choose up sides, and referee their own contests. Everything is organized by parents, every game is run by the referees—starting as early as age five. It shouldn't come as a surprise that so many kids come to view sports as just another form of regimentation. They're now more about performing for others and winning the game than they are about losing all track of time and running around with your buddies on a sunny Saturday morning.

I once saw a kids' soccer coach who could have served as a model for what ails youth sports. He blamed the referees for everything, and on a few occasions was ejected for his incessant harping. Humorless, tireless in his haranguing at his ten-year-old players, he acted as if each and every one of these little boys owed it to him to play like Pele.

Parents, to a shocking degree, aid and abet this madness. They consign their children to the care of these frustrated heroes, as mothers and fathers of previous generations gave their sons over to sadistic army drill sergeants. But those parents had had no choice.

If I had my choice to exercise all over again, I would help my sons organize games of their own. I would invite other fathers and sons over to play touch football or soft-ball. I wouldn't fight them if they decided they wanted to play in the organized leagues, but I wouldn't haul them there as soon as they were able to run. I certainly wouldn't repeat my mistake of urging them to play youth hockey at age five. I thought I was doing them a favor. For a time, it seemed that I was. They became great little skaters, and clearly loved to play. But then, all too soon, they were on traveling teams. We logged hundreds of miles driving to cold, out-of-the-way rinks. Our weekends were full. The boys began carefully keeping track of their actual minutes on the ice, begrudged the playing time of others, and remembered only whether they had won or lost.

The last thing I wanted was for Colin and McLean to associate golf with that sort of obligation. I didn't want them playing to please me or to meet my expectations for them.

I had recently started reading John Feinstein's book *A Good Walk Spoiled*, an insider's look at life on the professional golf tour. I was moved by an anecdote Feinstein shared about the relationship between Davis Love III and his father, a teaching golf professional.

Love senior had been extremely thorough in the instruction of his son. On nights after the two had played a round together, the father would share pages of notes on practically every shot his son had made as he moved around the golf course. He would question his son's strategy as well as the way he actually played the shots. But later in life, after Davis Love III had established himself as a successful touring professional, his father approached him with a single, simple question: He wanted to know if his son still loved the game. The son was perplexed, and protested that he loved the game as much as ever. Love senior wasn't convinced; he'd noticed something missing in the younger man's performance. He said it might be time for the son to find a new teacher, someone who could rekindle his passion to play.

That love has to be the most important consideration to every father as he guides his children toward their futures. If our children can't bring zest to the significant enterprises of their lives, they have every chance of becoming intimate with disappointment.

That's why I never even put the Jack Nicklaus instructional video into our VCR, and that's why I decided to get Colin and McLean out onto the golf course sooner than I had intended. My original game plan called for them to have at least five or six sessions at the range before we ventured across the street into the state park. When Nicklaus started playing at age ten, it was three months before he played his first nine holes—and shot 51. By age eleven, he'd shot an 81. At age twelve, he shot a 74. How could you argue with those types of results?

Actually, it was quite easy to take a different approach. My boys were so excited to play, that to deny them would have been counterproductive. That was just something I knew in my heart.

However, I would not have relented had we not had the par-three course at our disposal. To play the long eighteen-hole course would have been too much. The short course could provide the kindly illusion of success necessary to nurture the beginner.

*

We took our first step up to the tee at 6:30 P.M. on the Friday evening of Memorial Day weekend. The skies were threatening, but the trembling that the three of us felt was entirely of our own making.

I gave each of the boys two new balls, instructing them to watch their shots carefully and take clear mental note of where they landed. I was concerned that we might easily spend all of our time searching for lost balls.

By the time we reached the second green, I felt like a sheepherder. I'd traipse off in one direction to help McLean locate his ball and point him in the direction of the green, before hurrying back over to Colin, all the while trying to check their exuberance just enough to have them play in turn.

In their view, whoever was ready first should shoot away, whether he was farthest from the hole or not. I must admit here to having mixed feelings about enforcing the farthest-away-shoots-first-rule, because golf today is so often played so tediously. It's horrifying how many rounds take longer than four hours to complete. When we were kids, we would play a foursome around in three to three and a half hours. But, in this case, I was struggling against the threat of chaos. My little sheep were all over the lot.

Over the first several holes, Colin and McLean played an erratic game. One good shot, as far as they were concerned, made up for several flubs. The three of us were like happy drunks on a lark, choosing to exalt what went well and simply ignore what did not.

At the short fifth hole, however, there was a barely perceptible but significant shift in their attitudes. As the boys approached the tee and noticed that the hole was only ninety-three yards long, they acquired a sense of purpose that had been absent up to this point. Each had, during those four previous holes, hit at least a few shots that, if duplicated on this very short hole, would land them on the green in one. This realization inspired concentration and ignited their competitive fires. In other words, they settled down and began to pay attention.

Both of them missed the green, Colin over the back and McLean pin high to the left. But Colin made 4, his brother 6, and a more serious battle with the game now commenced.

Two holes later, on the 128-yard seventh, Colin hit a driver six feet to the right of the pin. Had anyone witnessed his jumping and hollering and general carrying on, they would have figured a hole in one. As far as Colin was concerned, it *was* a hole in one. It was his first green in regulation. It hardly mattered to him that he left the putt for birdie hanging on the lip, because he made his par and couldn't have been more pleased.

Ah, I thought to myself, *sweet innocence.* It wouldn't be long before a par would be cause for a sigh of relief rather than celebration.

But this was all about the discovery of control, and the will to play well. They were finally into playing the game, and while I had always assumed that would be the case, I was thankful that it had happened so effortlessly and imperceptibly to them.

By the time we finished nine holes, it was raining steadily and becoming chilly enough for me to be ready to quit. Since I'd driven straight from the office to meet the boys, I was also very hungry.

My sons were of a different mind.

"Come on, Dad," McLean protested. "Don't be a wimp. We're hungry, too, but we can handle it."

"This is too much fun," Colin said, hitting upon a much more powerful theme. "We can't stop now."

We didn't. And as we walked out onto the first tee for the second time, we saw a rainbow. It arched high across the sky in bands of color as vibrant and as solid as I'd seen in years.

"That's good luck, boys," I told them. "I think our experience together with golf is going to be full of good luck."

But I wondered whether that would prove to be true. My personal stake in our playing golf together was so great. I might be setting myself up for disappointment, setting them up in turn. Would I be open to letting Colin and McLean have their own experiences? I'd need to be on the lookout for signs that I was becoming overbearing, obscuring what might provide them inspiration to realize their own dreams.

The pupil or prospective learner cannot possibly direct his swing through a complete sequence of correct positions as ordered by the teacher. The whole thing happens too fast to be subject to this degree of conscious control. Nevertheless, since the successful player must have a good understanding of his swing, he must be made aware of the results to be expected from all conceivable movements, right or wrong.

—BOBBY JONES

✳

3

*

PAYING ATTENTION

In the weeks that followed, we alternated playing golf on Friday and Saturday evenings, also alternating between the par-three course and the eighteen-hole, par-seventy-two track. Once I had introduced the boys to the long course, they never wanted to play the par three again, since this was like being asked to go back a grade. But there were nights when I simply didn't have the stamina to face the par fours and fives. One of the boys seemed always to be enduring a ten- or eleven-stroke hole, and the cheerleading could be exhausting.

I was also conscious of the fact that our adventures on the eighteen-hole course were threatening to overwhelm the learning process. Negotiating doglegs, trying to hit the ball over water hazards, enduring long par fives, the boys would get caught up in mere survival. Making a good swing or lining up a putt properly often seemed like a trivial pursuit. When I would see this happening, I made sure our next round was played over at the par three, where the emphasis was much more on shot making.

Because morale does become so major an issue when teaching golf, I tried to keep in mind the great psychological lift of achieving a low score. With youth it usually doesn't matter whether that low score is obtained on a long or short hole. They simply love seeing the three, four, or five on the scorecard. Likewise, I had the sense to tell my sons that the ladies' tees were the juniors' tees, as well. I had made the mistake during our first trip around the eighteen-hole course of having them hit off the white tees with me, which made the holes much too long for them. The next time out they fought me when I made them hit from the reds, wounded that I would treat them like sissies, but from that day forward they embraced these "juniors' tees" as their god-given right to advantage.

No matter which course we played, I felt as if I was playing three balls of my own. Every time Colin and McLean prepared to hit, I was fixed on them, willing them to make a good swing, to keep their heads down and follow through. And with the execution of each shot I shared their feelings of triumph or frustration.

Sometimes, when it seemed as if they weren't making much progress, when they really hacked it up and the divots felt like chunks stripped from my own hide, they would surprise me by putting together two or three good shots in a row. This is how it goes in golf, and I knew I needed to smile, make gentle encouragement, and walk blithely ahead. While this is what I appeared to do, inwardly I was concerned.

What was troubling was the boys' lack of attention. Although they weren't actually goofing around, or thinking about being off somewhere else with their friends, they were not taking enough notice of how the way they made a swing or executed a putting stroke determined where the ball ended up.

Really paying attention means being in the moment completely enough to see the relationship between cause and effect. Typically kids are in the moment only as it pertains to how much fun they're having. They're not inclined to consider how their actions in the present might affect their futures.

By now, we had established with sufficient certainty that Colin and McLean both enjoyed golf, and I would always be careful not to forget the primacy of joy in the experience of the game, but I knew that if they were to establish a lasting relationship with golf they would need to respect its demand for full attention. Otherwise the game would become much too frustrating.

This process is much the same as that of growing up and learning what it takes to put together a fulfilling life. Attaining maturity might be viewed as bidding farewell to a world in which food, shoes, and days at the beach seem to just materialize before us. It's when we take our first conscious steps into a world where we must make things happen for ourselves. We begin to recognize how our actions trigger events and chains of events. It's also the time when we see that we must make our own luck.

People who know that we make our own luck are alert to their surroundings. They listen attentively and watch carefully. They monitor their own behavior to determine what produces the results they're looking for and what does not. They take responsibility for their own lives and are not devastated by failure. These are the people who don't easily give up, because they feel in control of their destinies.

This concept of the importance of paying complete attention can be a tough sell, especially when the audience is a couple of young boys expert in the art of having fun and little interested in compromising this art. I had suggested to Colin earlier in the summer, for example, that if he made an effort to read more books, he'd find ninth grade less intimidating. But he was unimpressed by the logic, and eventually I had to impose a six-book summer reading requirement if he wanted to play fall sports.

I was having equally little success in convincing Colin and McLean that golf is no more and no less than a string of consequences. I explained that if you didn't take the time to consider the speed of a downhill putt, you didn't just miss that particular putt, but usually placed the next putt in jeopardy, as well. After a three-putt hole, there is a natural inclination to overswing at the next tee and send the ball rocketing off into the woods. If you aren't careful, this momentum of misery becomes never-ending. It's a rather obvious pitfall for those of us who have been brutalized before by inattention to our playing of the game, but it is of only passing interest to a youth who thinks that there will always be time to set things right later.

I was in the midst of this quandary over how to make this point about the importance of paying attention when I spotted an announcement in the local paper one morning for the upcoming LPGA tournament at nearby Stratton Mountain, Vermont. At once, I saw this as the ideal opportunity: The pros play the game with an excruciating attention to everything, a trait that would be nearly impossible for my sons to overlook or not appreciate.

✵

In the hearts and minds of people who live in Saratoga, the McCall's LPGA Classic at Stratton Mountain Country Club, Vermont, had become the Dottie Pepper Classic, for it was their one chance each year to see the hometown hero in action.

Since moving to the area several years earlier I had been following Dottie's career as it was reverently chronicled in the daily newspaper, the *Saratogian*. I knew she first learned golf at age eight, taking a series of lessons at Murphy's driving range. From the beginning, she showed natural talent, but it was the same drive and dedication that she brought to her piano lessons, skiing, and just about everything else she did that would set her on the path to golfing stardom. Her incredible willingness to practice quickly became part of local lore. Courted by a coach who heard stories of the young girl who could play as well as the men, Dottie was given a special exemption to play on the boy's golf team at Saratoga High. A member of the varsity in the eighth grade, by tenth grade she was the team's number one player. At fifteen she won the New York State Women's Amateur Championship.

Much of the reporting about Dottie's career also mentioned the special relationship she had with an elderly golf professional at the nearby McGregor Links course.

"George Pulver," Dottie's high school coach was quoted as saying, "was her golfing dad."

In his early eighties when they were introduced, Pulver had recently lost his wife of sixty years and was a man suddenly without purpose. Young Dottie had already learned all she could about golf from everybody else around. Their coming together was the obvious handiwork of destiny.

As has been told in any number of feature articles, Pulver, after each lesson with his star pupil, would go home to his typewriter and compose a summary of what he and Dottie had gone over that day, being careful to include bits of wisdom about golf and life. Later, he would drive by Dottie's house and leave these thoughts tucked in the family's mailbox. Dottie would gather them in a notebook, and to this day refers to them when in search of guidance and inspiration. "He was everything to me," she has explained.

My knowledge of the local hero also included accounts of her legendary temper. Competitive to a fault, Dottie had been known to rage on the golf course. Following a Stratton Mountain LPGA tournament four years earlier, the *Saratogian* had been moved to admonish her in its lead editorial. The paper suggested that Dottie was prone to behaving like a brat whenever things weren't going her way and, while noting that the pressures of professional golf are considerable, lamented that she spent far too little time practicing her smile.

I expected that Dottie Pepper would provide us with any number of thrills and chills as we took a look at golf as played by those who depend upon it for their livelihood.

*

The weather forecast was dismal, but the boys and I made the winding seventy-five-mile drive over the mountains and into the Vermont National Forest without encountering any rain. There was little traffic to slow us, and we talked about dreams we had for our lives. McLean said that one day he'd like to have a house on the ocean in Hawaii, while Colin preferred to follow the seasons and ski and surf his way around the world. I admitted that if I could have a home on a beautiful golf course alongside the Atlantic I would know I was in the land of the happily-ever-after.

I was becoming much better at listening to my sons

talk about their lives away from me without feeling pangs of loneliness. For more than a year after their mother and I had separated, my attachment to them had been frightening—this despite a joint custody agreement that was remarkably agreeable. Because their mother worked Tuesday and Thursday nights, I had the boys these two times during the week, and then for large chunks of time over the weekend. On paper, this seemed a more than satisfactory arrangement, but in my heart it was anything but. I remember nights alone when I would go into their empty room and curl up on McLean's bottom bunk, finding that among traces of him, by being surrounded by their few possessions, I could breathe more easily.

I felt I had steeled myself sufficiently against the probable pains of leaving my children's home, but it is impossible to anticipate the agony of such a separation. It felt to me in the dark hours that I was in danger of losing my children's love—not because they would wish it, or because I wouldn't do everything in my power to make my love known to them, but simply because I had allowed this to happen to us all. Could any of our explanations about how things just weren't working for their mother and me possibly justify this?

There was also the sheer physical need I had to be with my sons. I had never known such complete happiness until they had come into my life, and I needed to touch them often, to run my fingers through their hair to verify that I hadn't just dreamed both of them up.

Time did eventually restore my confidence. I found ways to feel contentment when they weren't around. I took great comfort in seeing that they could be happy. Both continued to do well in school, and neither became moody or rebellious. *If these two young guys can handle it, I would tell myself, then I had better well learn to handle it, too.*

But just as I worried about forfeiting my children's love, I was especially reluctant to impose discipline on them. For a period of time, I eagerly fulfilled their short-term needs, and didn't worry that I might make them lazy, ungrateful, or lacking in self-discipline. I was more a friend than a parent, a tactic I now regret. Children can make friends most anywhere. Only their parents can attend to the business of making them solid citizens of the world.

*

Coming up the mountain around the final corner and into view of the Stratton Mountain Country Club, we were thrilled by what lay before us. The fairways were very bright green, made greener still by the whitest sand traps I had ever seen, filled as they were with lime-stone. And the course was cradled in the steep slopes of the Stratton Mountain ski area that rose majestically above it.

I'd called earlier that morning and learned that Dottie teed off on the tenth hole at 12:20, but I had not accounted for the time it would take to park the car miles away and travel back by an old school bus.

After jumping off the bus we galloped like goats up the cart path running alongside the tenth hole, huffing and puffing by the time we reached the crowd at the eleventh. We caught up with Dottie Pepper on her second hole of the second round.

In a summer that was breaking all kinds of records around the Northeast for days without rain, the McCall's LPGA Classic had already lost one round to rain, and dark clouds still hovered over the course.

Dottie had hit her approach to the short par three about twenty-five feet past the pin. She was beginning the undeviating rituals of her putting routine when we inched our way up to the edge of the green at a point close to her ball.

After spending long minutes lining up the putt from all directions, she made two careful practice swings, wiped the blade of her putter, then tugged at her shirt near the right shoulder. Next, with her right hand firmly holding the putter in front of the ball, she placed her left hand on her left thigh. Finally, she lifted the putter with her right hand back behind the ball and placed her left hand on the grip. She widened her stance, settled into place, and putted.

That first putt we watched was a very difficult one, first breaking left, then right, picking up speed rapidly as it worked downhill toward the cup. When it disappeared into the hole, the crowd erupted, and Dottie raised both arms up in the air, pumping her fists in her trademark victory cheer.

I looked for the first time at the scoreboard carried by a young man standing across from us at the right edge of the green. I knew Dottie had started the day at three under. The placard indicated she was now four under, which meant she had birdied the tenth. Now she had birdied the eleventh. We were witnessing a charge. I looked over to see Colin and McLean still clapping along with the rest of the gallery. The tournament had attracted a strong field—Pat Bradley, Patty Sheehan, Meg Mallon, and Kelly Robbins—but the local favorite was commanding the largest following, and she was starting to ride its energy to the top of the leader board. Pat Bradley stood at minus eight, but as I watched Dottie marching toward the next tee I had a feeling the tournament was hers. This five-foot-six-inch figure of determination was finally going to win a tournament with her mother and father in the crowd.

Colin looked over at me and smiled.

"What a putt," I remarked.

He nodded his head, clearly impressed. Any concerns I had that he might be bored by watching the day's play disappeared.

McLean drew up alongside me. He was looking up at the ski slopes, way above us on the mountain top. "When we were skiing there last year, Dad," he said, "I didn't even notice the golf course."

"Probably because it was covered in snow," I suggested.

He considered that.

"And I didn't care about golf then," he added.

We followed Dottie Pepper for nine holes. She's not only consistent in her swing routines, she's consistently on target. Her iron shots were like darts thrown right at the pin, sticking to the soft, small greens.

"She's really good, isn't she?" Colin asked after we watched her hit a long, straight drive.

"She's got a great swing," I agreed.

"I like the way she looks at the end," Colin said. "I

like the way she's standing there with the club all the way around. She looks like a statue."

"Why don't you try imitating that?" I asked.

"I might," Colin replied.

What struck me was how conservatively Dottie played, though others might call it intelligently. As straight as she was hitting the ball, she was taking out irons on several par fours and fives. I was rarely able to resist pulling the driver from my bag. I vowed to imitate this aspect of Dottie's game.

It was on the sixteenth hole that we saw the Dottie Pepper who had once drawn the ire of her hometown newspaper. Just as she was completing her swing on her second shot, a long iron to the green, the nearby crowd surrounding the seventeenth green erupted in cheers and applause. Dottie hit her iron a little fat, and after seeing it land left and short, she herself erupted, slamming her club down on the ground and glaring over in the direction from where the cheers had come. If looks could kill, they were all dead over on the seventeenth.

Still visibly perturbed, Dottie chipped up to four feet. After taking what seemed an eternity to size up the putt, she missed, as the ball seemed to hop over a spike mark. Dottie let out a loud growl. After tapping in the remaining two-inch putt, she slammed her putter down on the offending spike mark and stormed off the green towards the next tee, steam billowing out of her ears.

"Did you see that?" Colin asked, as we trotted off toward the seventeenth green. "She went ballistic."

"Let's see if she can shake it off and get back to business," I said.

Her shot to the short seventeenth sailed right of the green. "She's got to get back in the moment," I observed to Colin and McLean.

"She's still really mad, Dad," McLean said.

"It appears so," I said. "But she's a pro. I'll bet you she pulls it back together here."

And she did. After getting down in two and salvaging par at 17, Dottie went on to birdie 18. Walking off the eighteenth green to cheers of encouragement, she even allowed herself a brief smile.

It was raining harder now, and the boys had had enough. We set sail for home. As we were crossing back over into New York, Colin said, "That was a really fun day, Dad. Thanks." This had the effect of a tough side-hill putt sneaking into my heart for birdie.

Had Colin and McLean learned anything from our golfing day-trip about the value of paying attention? Would they start concentrating more, and begin to evaluate how the way they played a shot produced a negative or positive result? It was hard to tell. Each of them had remarked at different times during the afternoon about how each of the professionals had her own set of idiosyncracies. Although they sometimes found these habitual behaviors funny, I knew they would try to imitate a few of them because they had been impressed by how straight and true these women hit the ball. They both commented about how well the women all putted.

They had also witnessed golf as played to an adoring audience, which seemed to have the effect of making the game more significant and appealing to them. Until then, they might have suspected that I was one of the very few who cared much about golf. Its news was usually ignored by television newscasters, and only a couple of their friends played with what seemed mild interest.

The next night on the local news I watched Dottie Pepper cry tears of joy as she accepted the winner's trophy in the company of her mother and father. I got a little choked up myself.

Turning the television off, I sat back in the chair and closed my eyes. I found myself thinking about Dottie's "golfing dad," George Pulver. What message might he write to me about my performance so far as a golf teacher? I'd never met the man, but I imagined that at his age, after all he'd seen and heard, his notes to Dottie were generous and to the point.

Don't be so hard on yourself, he might have written to me. *It's okay to be a little hard on them. Dottie made that part easy for me. The biggest challenge I had was getting her to relax and let go. The more she had to concentrate, the more she liked it. Your boys are good little players. They'll discover that if you play and think at the same time it ends up being a lot more fun. But they'll come to that in time. . . . How about my Dottie? She can play, can't she?*

I opened my eyes, and smiled.

"She can play, all right," I said out loud. "You did a good job, George."

The golf swing is far too complex to nail down to a science. Starting from a static position and swinging the club back, up and then down so that it strikes the ball squarely and solidly while traveling at great speed requires an extremely precise coordination of the mind and the body.

—SEVE BALLESTEROS

✯

4

✴

CONNECTING THE MIND AND BODY

It was two weeks after our trip to see the women professionals play that the boys and I finally had the chance to play golf again. Determined to keep the memories fresh, I reminded Colin on the first tee of the Spa course about developing some kind of routine to keep himself focused on his putting. While I didn't notice that he created any particular putting ritual, he did start crouching down behind the ball to line up his putts, something that he had never done before, and that led to a genuine improvement.

I also reminded McLean that we had all marveled at how Dottie Pepper never missed a shot, and that this seemed much more important than hitting the ball as far as possible. But McLean loved his big swing, and made no extra effort during that round to keep his ball in play.

When he hit the ball well it went soaring, and the pleasure he took in these successes was considerable. Much more often, though, he beat the ball into the ground, but these disasters were not enough to dissuade him from his walloping approach. What frustrated me was that he actually had a very good swing, and it was clear that if he would try bringing it under control, he might know a brand of golf familiar to a select few.

The young golfer especially should feel free to explore his or her natural swing. But the bigger the swing, the greater the need to get it into a well-worn groove. In general, when we go directly for the glory, we'd better be prepared to work a little harder than the rest. In golf, for every fellow who hits the ball hard and straight there are at least a thousand other guys who swing with all their might and are still waiting to hit their first fairway.

It's been said time and again that golf is a game of "feel." Doubtless it is. But feel doesn't fall from the heavens into the hands of the chosen few. Feel is the hard-earned result of thousands of hours on the practice tee or putting green. Young star Phil Mickelson is said to have the best putting touch of any player on earth. It should come as no surprise to learn that when he was a boy his father built a putting green in their backyard. Mickelson's magical touch is born of more hours of practice putting than the rest of us will do in a lifetime.

I had little expectation that McLean would spend hours at the practice range working on his swing. By nature he just wasn't so inclined, and his summer was filled with rollerblading expeditions around town with his pals, a vacation with his mother, and soccer camp. If he was ever going to succeed at golf, lacking the time and determination to grind away at the practice range for hours, he would need to become especially sensitive to the body-mind connection.

For children, achieving such a connection is a significant challenge. Characteristically, they tend to the extremes, fixed on either having fun, experiencing only bodily pleasures, or becoming unduly nervous and self-conscious, using their minds exclusively to worry. This was a pattern McLean followed almost to the letter when he was playing golf. He would either swing away with no concern at all about what he was doing, sending the ball off in every direction, or he would become tense and frustrated and would be practically unable to hit the ball at all. To play golf well and to engage in any physical activity successfully, it's almost as if we have to grow a little mind in our body, a mind separate from the brain.

We need to create a body memory so the body "knows" the feel of a good swing, so the body "remembers" what to do when it's standing over a delicate chip shot.

That's why as the summer progressed the boys and I had continued to go to Murphy's driving range at least once every couple of weeks. On certain evenings I would force them to stay with one club until they demonstrated consistent, solid contact, which sometimes meant that nearly the entire bucket would be gone before they could thrash away with their beloved drivers. Other times I would instruct them to think of nothing else except ending up with a beautiful follow-through, standing perfectly in position, as Dottie Pepper had.

But I knew that Colin and McLean still did not have a clue as to what caused them to hit the ball well one time and miss it the next. They weren't yet feeling a rhythm in their swings. They weren't concerned with tempo. They didn't think about controlling the swing path. They might as well have been in the baseball batting cage, swinging away at every pitch tossed in by the mechanical pitcher, delighted to make any kind of contact.

Colin and McLean had observed how Dottie Pepper paid very careful attention to everything she did on the golf course, and how her diligence resulted in a very impressive level of play. This was the rudimentary lesson in the subject of cause and effect. What my sons still didn't understand was how Dottie used her hours at the practice range to experience how the movements of her body affected the outcomes of her swings. Her paying attention had become internalized. With her mind commanding her body, she made an indelible imprint on its pattern of motions.

By the time a top golfing professional has left the practice range for the first tee, he or she is ready to consider a single "swing thought," and the body is ready to answer with an instinctive response. The pro walks up to a shot and, with a simple mental command, tells the body what it needs to do. The body just does it. The mind is the organizer, creating the mental image of where the shot should go, and the body takes it from there.

This project of making a solid mind-body connection is no mean feat, and it is exceedingly difficult to sustain over long periods of time. In fact, it seems to come in erratic bursts of energy. I don't remember Dottie Pepper coming close to winning a tournament in the weeks following the McCall's Classic, though she did continue to play much-better-than-average golf. Even on her bad days, the mind-body connection served her quite well.

But how does the beginner develop a swing that reflects a good working partnership between the mind and the body?

*

It was a Friday evening, and as we had gotten a late start for the golf course, we were entirely unprepared for the massive traffic jam we encountered at the entrance to the state park.

As well as its two golf courses, the park also accommodates the Saratoga Performing Arts Center, summer home to the New York City Ballet and the Philadelphia Orchestra, and a popular venue for a variety of rock-and-roll headliners. That night, Melissa Etheridge was appearing, and some twenty thousand people were flocking into the park to see her.

Determined to play golf, we swerved over into the breakdown lane, scurrying past the main entrance to the park, and into a bank parking lot a few hundred yards down the road. We knew that by the time we made it to the golf course daylight would be scarce, so we quickly alighted from the car, grabbed our golf bags out of the trunk, and started walking.

"I feel a little silly," Colin said, as, our bags slung over our shoulders, we passed vans loaded with young people listening to loud music and whooping it up in anticipation of the night's reveries.

I laughed, fully appreciating my son's discomfort. I've never really lost my own sense of teenage angst over appearing less than cool in public. Although we were dressed like members of the tribe—the boys in oversized T-shirts, long khaki shorts, scuffed-up indoor soccer shoes, and dirty baseball caps pulled down on their foreheads, and me wearing a faded old golf shirt with the buttons missing, baggy khaki pants, and aging running shoes—our golf bags must have made us seem especially uncool to the concertgoers, who were busy drinking beer and hanging out the car windows howling at the moon. Mercifully, it was only a few minutes before we could duck into a pathway through the woods where we could walk for a half-mile unobserved into the park.

By the time we reached the golf course, picking it up at the thirteenth tee, I noticed that the cars inching their way along the road into the park had turned on their headlights. We'd be lucky to get in a few holes before it became impossible to follow the flights of our balls. Caught up in the party atmosphere and the thrill of playing in the night, the boys joked and laughed with each other, something they did much too infrequently.

We had managed to play only two holes when the

Melissa Etheridge concert began. The sound carried easily from the open amphitheater, across the park, and down the fairways. We almost viscerally felt the roar of the crowd when the star took the stage and revved up the band. We could even make out most of the words as she began to sing.

McLean, a big Melissa Etheridge fan, had all her tapes and knew the lyrics to most of the songs. I heard him start singing as we walked the fourteenth fairway. Colin looked over at me and shook his head. He did not share his younger brother's passion for rock and roll and associated McLean's singing with the annoyance he felt when McLean played the stereo too loud in the bedroom at the break of day.

We were approaching the sixteenth tee when the distant crowd cheered as Ms. Etheridge launched into the opening of her big hit, "Come to My Window." Quickly, McLean's voice came in over the top of hers, singing the next line, "Wait by the light of the moon."

I chuckled, Colin groaned, and we both hit away.

"Get up there and hit," Colin ordered his brother, motioning toward the tee box. He was attempting to cut off McLean's singing and keep us moving in what little light remained to guide us.

Imperturbable, McLean continued to sing as he

pulled his driver from his bag and sashayed toward the tee markers. Slowly, intent upon tuning into the song, he pushed his tee into the ground, placed the ball atop its perch, and assumed his stance. When he appeared finally to be ready to hit away, he suddenly stopped, looking back in the direction of the music.

"This one's for you, Melissa," he called out. He then waggled his fanny in exaggeration, waggled his driver, and proceeded to make a great swing. The ball shot off into the darkening sky. It was one of the best drives of the summer, about 125 yards straight down the middle.

I couldn't stop laughing. Unable to fight it, Colin laughed, too. McLean, entirely satisfied, allowed himself just the merest hint of a ten-year-old's smile, picked up his bag, and went walking off after his ball, acting as if hitting it so far and so straight was just another in a series of perfect moments in his golfing life.

That night, lying in bed, I was recalling that moment and chuckling to myself when it occurred to me that we might use McLean's impromptu waggle to his advantage. Just days before, I had been reading a book by the esteemed golfing instructor David Leadbetter, who advised that establishing a bit of a waggle during the setup for a swing could be very helpful. It diffuses the tension in the body, Leadbetter said, and gives us a sense of the club in our hands, thus making us more inclined to get the entire body into the swing rather than just the arms and hands.

McLean did have a tendency to tense up over the ball. But more than merely relaxing him, I hoped that by urging him to make a little waggle with his fanny and his clubhead as he was getting ready to make his swing, he would adopt it as his own ritual that would focus him in the moment. This would start him thinking about how he needed to get his body ready to hit the ball where his mind wanted it to go.

I didn't get much sleep that night. Initially it was due to my excitement over finding a method I might use to help McLean improve his golf, but afterward, it was my greater concern that McLean's approach to golf was all too typical of the way he approached life. He was not inclined to work at things that didn't come easily. He didn't pursue any activities at which he didn't show immediate promise. So far there had been enough that had come naturally to him to keep him satisfied. He didn't yet realize that achievement is usually the result of working hard to overcome the odds. He was still given to believe that things just "happen."

It did seem at times that McLean lived a charmed existence, as if a guardian angel hovered protectively over him, giving him the goose whenever he really needed to be at his best. That's certainly how it seemed the day very early in the summer when I enrolled him and Colin in a special junior golf day program at the Spa Park. My primary intention had been to have McLean discover for himself that his golf swing was not the stuff of legend, but my intentions had been decidedly foiled.

*

I had seen in the *Saratogian* that the Northeast PGA was sponsoring a free clinic for junior golfers at the Spa course. The kids would receive instruction from PGA professionals, and in addition would be treated to an exhibition by a man who was paralyzed from the waist down, but who could hit an array of trick golf shots and play the game very well. This, to me, sounded like a wonderful morning.

McLean's reaction to my description of the program was immediately negative. "A lesson?" he said. "That sounds pretty boring, Dad."

"This is a great opportunity," I insisted energetically. "One of these pros may give you just the tip you need to become really good."

"What do you think, Colin?" I asked, turning my attention to my more responsive student. "Sound good to you?"

When he hesitated, I took the offensive.

"Oh, I get it," I said sarcastically. "You two are already so good that a professional can't tell you a thing."

"That's not it," Colin complained. "It sounds like a lot of kids and a lot of standing around."

"I won't know anybody," McLean added.

"So what?" I said, cheerleading again. "You'll know each other. So what if you don't know anybody? This is a great opportunity. And what about this exhibition? The guy is a paraplegic and he's still a great golfer. I'm going to try to get away from the office for a little while and see that part for myself. I'll drop you off for the instruction period and then come back in time for the exhibition."

I hardly gave them a choice. For two days, depending upon my state of mind, I either cajoled them or dressed them down for their arrogance in refusing to recognize a great opportunity. For my own part, I expected to be thrilled and inspired by the "The Dennis Walters Golf Show."

"The Dennis Walters Golf Show" is Dennis, paralyzed by a golf cart accident in 1974; his father, Bucky; and his dog, Mulligan. Dennis, of course, is the star. Once a golfer accomplished enough to win the New Jersey State Juniors Championship and finish eleventh in the U.S. Amateur Championship, he had first assumed that as a result of his accident he would never play golf again. But after months spent in the hospital and in excruciating therapy and physical rehabilitation, he found that he was determined to find a way to play the game that had always been such a joyful part of his life. Allying ingenuity to his fierce determination, he retrofitted a golf cart so that the passenger seat would swivel to the side. Held in place by a seat belt, he could swing at the ball, using just his upper body. When it came time to putt, he would raise himself up on crutches. In time, in addition to learning to play in this fashion well enough to consistently break 40 for nine holes (and shoot two holes in one), Dennis became accomplished at a variety of trick shots. Encouraged by others, he had taken his show on the road.

When I arrived at the exhibition, Dennis was hitting drives with a pretty little hook about 225 yards dead straight down the practice range. Then he showed the crowd of about a hundred kids and a smattering of parents how he could hit three balls with one swing, hit beautiful shots with a rubber-shafted club, hit blindfolded, and hit in rapid-fire succession balls rolled at him down a makeshift ramp of golf clubs.

Dennis's father teed up the balls. Occasionally, Mulligan jumped into the act, also teeing up the ball or running to fetch the short shots. Throughout his performance, Dennis maintained a dialogue with the kids.

"If there is one thought I'd like you to come away with today," Dennis remarked as he set up his final shot, "it is that when you get in some situation where you really want to do something and everybody tells you it's impossible to do, remember the guy who was paralyzed and figured out a way to continue playing the game he loved."

While I knew I'd remember that lesson for a long time, I worried that my sons might not, because at the conclusion of the exhibition they were running headlong over to where free hot dogs and sodas had been set up. When I caught up with them, all they wanted to say, talking between bites, was how they had fared in the competitions they'd participated in after the instruction sessions. McLean had won a golf ball in the putting contest.

I wanted to know what the pros had said about their swings. Colin told me they had adjusted his grip, because he had a weak left hand. He'd used the stronger grip, and it had made an immediate difference. McLean said that when the pro walked up behind him, he hit his best shot of the day.

"The pro said it didn't look like I needed any help at all," McLean boasted, swelling his chest out.

Weeks later, as I lay awake in the middle of the night, I was still confused about what I should do. If McLean was comfortably breezing along through life, did I really want to catch him up short? For the longest time I had been pleased to think that he was developing a healthy self-esteem, but I worried now that the fates might be setting him up for some particularly vexing problems later on—ones he would be ill prepared to deal with.

What parent doesn't want his child to live in a state of eternal bliss, shielded from life's harsh truths, ignorant of how difficult it is to realize our dreams? Even before I had children of my own, I loved the fictional character of Garp. I cheered wildly as I read in *The World According to Garp* the chapter in which Garp goes running through the streets of his cozy suburban neighborhood, attempting to chase down speeders and admonish them that there were innocent children playing, children who might wander out in the street and get run down by irresponsible adults. Garp was desperate to keep his children from all harm in a reckless universe. But were I to read this book now, I would admonish Garp that his time would be better spent instructing his children on how people often drive like fools, and that they should approach the road with fear and trembling. If I have learned anything with the passage of time, it is that those who live long are those who learn to recognize harm and stay out of its way. I believe the greatest gift I can give my children is to teach them self-responsibility and self-awareness.

I also know that children are not inclined to welcome such counsel, and that extra efforts are often required to have them seriously heed the advice. They don't want to hear that those who become truly intimate with defeat, those who look closely enough to see that defeat is often a wake-up call and an opportunity to accept the lesson and move on to the next level, are those who achieve real success in life. I'd been reading studies showing that children who have their needs met on demand, children who don't come to understand that we often must delay short-term satisfaction in favor of working for something in the future of greater and lasting quality, are less likely to become adults with satisfying careers and lives.

Like Garp, I had spent too much time when McLean was a little boy doing more applauding of his successes than helping him overcome his defeats. He was not at all practiced in the art of humility. His natural speed made him stand out in soccer, for example, and masked his neglect of sound dribbling and passing skills. He was not, as far as I could tell, developing strong willpower. He was easily frustrated. He was reluctant to find the limits of his capabilities.

When we do only what comes easily, we can never benefit from the experience of willing ourselves to reach beyond what seems immediately possible to one day achieve something that lies beyond our grasp. In golf, strong willpower is an absolutely essential requirement for excellence. In golf, we must, quite literally, will the ball where we want it to go. Stories are legend among professional golfers about moments when they or others they were playing with willed a putt into the hole. We amateurs are also well aware that if we don't keep our minds focused on the job at hand we can't play very well at all.

Jack Nicklaus has long been considered golf's supreme competitor. Many observers have spoken of how his concentration, his will to win, is something they can actually feel in his presence. Many of his opponents over the years have experienced this force as fierce and intimidating. Others react with a sense of awe. But what's instructive is to consider how Jack Nicklaus himself feels in these moments when his will takes over. According to his books, as well as to interviews he's given over the years, he is so entirely consumed by his thoughts about getting the job done that he feels relatively little outside pressure. His determination to achieve the goal dominates the moment.

Similar stories are told about Ben Hogan—about how he didn't hear crowd noises on the golf course. About how he occasionally had no idea who it was that was threatening his lead as he played the final holes of a championship. He was in his own world, hearing and attending to only the uninterrupted instructions of his own mind.

When all the mental dials are locked in, the emotions and the feelings of doubt get locked out. The body is not receiving conflicting messages, and is freed to do its thing. I was hoping that the waggle would help McLean get dialed in. If he would make a conscious effort to make this movement each time he prepared to make a swing, it would become a signal that mind and body were preparing to work together, and that no distractions were tolerated.

If McLean would remember the night when he first waggled for Melissa and hit the ball so well, he would also have a clear and positive mental picture. This idea of forming an image of where we want to go also plays a critical role in golf. Again, Jack Nicklaus provides an extreme example. He claims that before each shot he actually sees the ball in flight, sees it land right where he wants it to land. He describes this as a vision as clear and as vivid as any that might be experienced by a mystic having a vision of paradise.

As I finally drifted off to sleep that night, I felt hopeful that, while I probably hadn't found the key to creating the next Nicklaus, I might have found the key to finding the maximum McLean.

✻

At the start of our next round at the Saratoga Spa course, as we waited alongside the first tee for our turn to play, I took McLean aside.

"Remember that night we played during the Melissa Etheridge concert?" I said.

He nodded.

"Remember how on the sixteenth tee you said, 'This one's for you, Melissa,' shook your butt, and then knocked it way out there in the fairway?"

He smiled and looked down, the color rising in his cheeks. "Yeah, I remember."

111
✻

"Well, I want you to waggle your butt like that when you stand up to hit every drive today."

"You want me to shake my butt?" he asked incredulously.

"Yes. Just like you did that night," I repeated. "And when you do it, think about how you hit it that night, think about how straight and far it went."

"Okay," he said, though he hardly sounded convinced. He shrugged as he moved over to his bag and reached for his driver.

McLean was careful to waggle on nearly every drive that day, as well as on many of his iron shots, and he hit the ball with improved consistency. These results were not dramatic; his game was still marked by wild fluctuations. But in the weeks that followed, as I watched him waggle, I witnessed him taking greater care with his approach to the game. He began to bear down. His demeanor was more determined.

This determination was ratcheted up, no doubt, by the performance of his older brother. Colin had begun to use his five-iron off the tee, and not only was this keeping him in play, but as his confidence in the middle iron increased, so, too, did his proficiency with it. I had tried for a time earlier in the summer to encourage this practice of hitting irons exclusively but had been met with more resistance than I was prepared to meet. Now, having reached this conclusion on his own, Colin was delighted to own the fairway.

McLean would never give up on his driver, but he knew that he would need to bear down and pay attention to what he was doing or risk too much embarrassment when we were tallying up the scores. If the baser instincts of sibling rivalry would serve my cause, I concluded, then I would accept them for now.

We were reaching a critical moment. We'd run through the basics, we'd put the game in focus. They were players now. But would they come to genuinely love to play? And if so, could they make this a sustaining love, one that might last a lifetime? I was eager to discover the answers to these questions as much for my own sake as for the boys'.

When we're together on the course, we're all at the mercy of the winds and the grass and our own frailties, and none of this stuff between people—the racial tensions, the upper/lower-class boundaries, the political or religious differences—makes a damn bit of difference.

—CHARLIE SIFFORD

✤

5

*

PLAYING TOGETHER

It's often said that the most meaningful measurement of golf is against the self, not others. In recognizing this truth that would appear to be so self-evident we shouldn't underestimate its considerable demands. When we compete against the self, losing our cool leaves us as goners. If we can't maintain calm, the results are calamitous. When we compete against the self, if we don't rivet our attention on the task at hand we usually wind up looking ridiculous.

That's why golfers are so often inclined to help one another, cheer each other on, sometimes even under match conditions. We all appreciate how enormous a task it is to measure up against the self, and are entirely empathic to anyone battling to maintain composure, to restore equilibrium.

That's why golf is a game as much about the camaraderie, the walk together, as it is about flailing away at that little dimpled ball. Because on the golf course we are respectful of the struggle others make to stay calm in the face of adversity. We know how hard it is to be focused when the mind is inclined to recall a million helpful tips, or to intrude with recollections of problems at home or at the office.

That's why golf encourages courtesy and thoughtfulness, and why golfers, for example, are so careful on the greens not to walk across another player's line, realizing that even the smallest indentation made by a spike mark can send a ball hopping in the wrong direction. We all know so well how difficult it is to succeed in the battle against the self, that we have no desire to increase that difficulty for others.

Those of us who have been playing the game for years have also discovered that in extending goodwill to our fellow players, and in receiving their own in return, our travails are made bearable and our triumphs increase in pleasure. This becomes something of a lesson in love; we see that by extending ourselves we are rewarded with something very positive.

But children can all too easily become accustomed to living exclusively on the receiving end. Of course, that's how, of necessity, they start out in the world, and for years they find no good reason to have it be any other way. They can remain quite content thinking only of others giving to them. My sons, for example, spent most of the summer hearing me applaud every good shot they made, and yet rarely did they think to cheer my better moments.

Usually, I brushed their indifference off. It's unseemly to seek praise, I reminded myself, even for a father simply asking a son to be generous of spirit. It's also easy to forgive our children when they see us as serene in our confidence and thus not in need of praise. After all, we work tirelessly to project this air of tranquility. But even after I buoyed myself with such arguments there were times when my sons' failure to give me a little pat couldn't be overlooked. Twice while playing the par-three course in the Spa Park I put my tee shots within just a couple of feet of the hole for tap-in birdies. Both times I waited for a reaction and then finally said, "You guys might want to say 'Nice shot.' I did practically put it in the hole just then!"

In general, I wasn't playing very well this summer, and I savored such small victories. But the boys just sort of chuckled, not considering that I might really appreciate some applause. They did not yet understand the reciprocal nature of friendship as so admirably practiced on golf courses everywhere. They regarded me exclusively as coach, and because I seemed to pay much more attention to their games than my own, they saw no reason to offer me solace against the game's difficult demands. Observing this, I realized they were lacking an important lesson in golf, and in life. I knew as well that the lesson would require some intervention from outside our little family unit.

On a number of occasions during the summer we had the opportunity to be joined by a fourth, and there were also opportunities when I was playing with either Colin or McLean alone when we might have hooked up with another twosome. Each time, the boys confided that they would rather not play in the company of strangers. I respected those feelings, and never forced the issue. But because they expressed no such reticence when presented with the chance to play with members of my family, it was these games with my father and my brothers that became their entryway into the more magical realms of golf, where they would learn the powerful two-way connections we can make with others, and find in that communion a direct incitement of the spirit to carry on.

*

That summer we played the "Shanley Tournament" earlier than was our custom. Usually my twin brothers, Brian and Paul, seven years my junior; my father; and I got together in the middle of August. But looking at his calendar after the second weekend in July, Brian couldn't see another opening. Brian is a Catholic priest in the Dominican Order, and it has long been held in our family that while we all remained staggered by his sacrifice of celibacy, Brian certainly seemed to have designed himself an enviable life, allowing ample time for study and contemplation as well as time to absorb the *New York Times* each day, freed from the routine frenzy of family living. After an evening baby-sitting for his nieces or nephews, he would heartily concur. But he'd recently accepted a teaching appointment at Catholic University and demands upon his time were multiplying.

Brian's twin, Paul, was a policeman. With both a priest and a cop in the family, the Shanleys had been indelibly stamped as Irish Catholic. Paul, a lieutenant on the Warwick, Rhode Island, police force, had never strayed far from home. He protected the old neighborhood with the very mixture of common sense and compassion we would hope for in a cop. Brian and Paul didn't look very much alike, but they were quite a pair. Colin and McLean sometimes referred to their Uncle Brian as the "ninja priest." At five feet nine inches, he was built like a little Charles Atlas. He was an avid weightlifter and had been a practitioner of the martial arts for years. Since he also ran a few miles a day, I figured he had to be the fittest cleric in the country. Paul, the biggest of the Shanley boys at six feet and 190 pounds, also lifted weights and practiced the martial arts. He once playfully picked me up in a big wrestler's bear hug, leaving my ribs sore for days. My mother must have discovered vitamin supplements after my brother Michael and I were born, as we've both been thin all our lives.

The Shanley Tournament was often the only time all year when Brian and Paul, my father, and I got together and played golf, competing and celebrating the one thing we all loved most after God, family, and friends. You might think then that I would have respected the moment enough to have fully prepared myself for its considerable demands upon my psyche. And yet as I left for Rhode Island I did so with the full knowledge that I had yet to play a complete eighteen-hole round, fully believing that this wouldn't matter. After two nights of hitting the ball very well at Murphy's driving range, I had announced myself sufficiently prepared to defend my title. The previous summer I had shot a 78, a round that included my first eagle, the result of holing out a three-wood from 225 yards on the difficult sixteenth hole. I could see no reason why I would not again vanquish my father and brothers.

While Colin was off on a trip with one of his pals, McLean had preceded me by a week to Rhode Island, spending time being spoiled by his grandmother and grandfather and playing golf with them twice. He called me the night before I left to join him, to tell me how that afternoon he had hit it across the water on the par-three ninth hole at Warwick Country Club, a feat I had warned him might be beyond his abilities and a feat his grandmother had informed him she never took for granted even after twenty-five years of playing the water hole. He also wanted to let me know that he had driven the cart for his grandmother—fully aware that I thought golf carts were forged from the fires of hell—and that he'd gotten as big a charge out of this ride as he'd thought he would.

McLean also told me that his grandfather had taught him a lot of important details about golf that week—how to tend the flagstick, how to rake out a sandtrap, how to be careful not to make noise when someone else was hitting, even if it was someone on another fairway. I had tried to convey these very same lessons myself, but apparently my father had had more success in making a real impression. I was grateful. I had hoped my father's reverence for the game would rub off, and I was delighted to hear that it was doing so quickly.

I stood on the first tee at Warwick Country Club on that sunny Friday morning after I arrived, diamonds of light sparkling on the surface of Narragansett Bay to my right, the first fairway stretching out in front of me in a perfect carpet of emerald green. It had been nearly a year since I'd visited there, and I was immediately lifted from my shoes and floated up to where I could survey the entire domain and my place in it.

When I was a teenager, Warwick Country Club was my sanctuary in a world I often found impersonal and chaotic. I got to know so many people there, and we called each other by name. There was a hierarchy, and I understood its logic. On the golf course, the better players were treated with deference, while everywhere else, it was the elders who were accorded privilege, even those whose idiosyncratic behavior sometimes caused tittering among us.

This was a friendly world. For the most part members left behind their pretensions when they made the final turn off Warwick Neck Avenue, reduced their speed as they entered under the canopy of trees above the road that ran alongside the twelfth hole, and fixed their attentions on the placement of the flagsticks, wondering over the speed of the greens. They had nothing to fret about now. Nothing the least violent would occur, other than the infrequent club thrown into the bushes. When they alighted from the locker room, they would be happily feathered in lime green, pink, and bright madras. I knew these were the captains of industry, mayors, and surgeons, but when I was their caddy and they leaned in to hear my recommendations on their next shot, they were always respectful and attentive.

Later, during my college years, I began to question the exclusivity of country club life. All its members were white. The yearly dues were not designed to accommodate the budget of the average wage earner. Yet in all my time there I never heard it suggested that our membership entitled us to feel in any way superior. The sense I got, rather, was that we should consider ourselves fortunate to simply be there. Because being there was the thing. The Englishman had his garden, the lovers their walk in the park. We had this abundance of green land jutting out into the bay, looking out to the ocean. No one felt more fortunate to be there than I.

As I stepped onto the course that morning of the

Shanley Tournament I reminded myself to cherish this thought, this privileged vision of peace and contentment, no matter what happened over the next four hours of play.

But as soon as I three-putted the third hole for a double bogey, I immediately began to press, and the battle was lost. I managed two birdies, and during a stretch of six holes on the backside I was even par, but mostly I played very messy golf, finishing double bogey, double bogey for an 87.

My father won the tournament easily, though neither he nor Brian nor Paul played particularly well. Sometimes poor play grips an entire foursome, and we become like survivors of a shipwreck, clinging to the pieces of the wreckage, encouraging one another to hold tight until help arrives.

McLean, on the other hand, thought the Shanley Tournament was a jolly good show. From his vantage point as caddie, he watched his father humbled, listened to his Uncle Brian calling out to the heavens in ways wildly different from his Sunday sermons, and saw Paul on the fourth hole hit a very low liner from the men's tees that smacked into one of the ladies' tee markers and disappeared. It was just one of those days, and McLean couldn't stop talking about it.

"Where do you think Uncle Paul's ball went?" he asked me a full month later. "Do you think it could have shot up into one of the trees next to the tee and just stayed there?"

"Not likely," I replied, "though anything's possible, I suppose."

"It couldn't have gone that far," he insisted.

Actually, it could have. Paul had made very solid contact, and the ball had not only knocked the ladies' red marker from its moorings but left a harsh white stain in its wake.

"Why do you keep reminding me of that dreadful day?" I said, morosely.

"Do you remember Paul's next shot?" he asked, smiling. "He hit it over into that sand trap next to the seventh green."

"I don't think your Uncle Paul would be very happy to know that you're still talking about this," I said.

"He sure was mad, wasn't he?"

"He was," I concurred. "But he made amends the next day, didn't he?"

"Do you think he played so well at Swansea because he was still mad about losing that ball?"

"No, I don't think that was it," I said. "I think it was your play that inspired him."

While McLean considered that possibility, he looked away, scrunching up his face and drawing together the string of freckles across the top of his cheeks and the bridge of his nose.

"I did play good that day," he said bashfully, looking down, the corners of his mouth turning up.

"You sure did," I agreed.

✻

When we got back to my mother and father's house after the Shanley Tournament, Brian and I were unable to rinse out the sour taste of the day's poor play. We began calling around to golf courses, and were able to secure a 6:19 A.M. tee time the following morning at Swansea Country Club, a very good public course about twenty miles away, just across the Massachusetts state line. My father already had a match scheduled at his club, so this time Paul, Brian, and I would be joined as four with McLean.

Whereas the day before we had experienced the exclusive pleasures of private country club life—no waiting, lush fairways, and panoramic views—this was a day to enjoy workingman's golf. We were up at five and chomping on donuts and sipping strong coffee as we walked up to the first hole, drenched in early morning dew.

But if the scenery had changed, the quality of the golf had not—at least for me, it hadn't. I shot another 87, as inconsistency and erratic iron play continued to drive me crazy. I had three birdies, and a triple bogey on the easiest hole on the course.

Because I refused to acknowledge that my game was in shambles, on the first tee that morning I had challenged Brian and Paul to a five-dollar nassau. Their best ball against me. After nine I was three down. Paul was having the round of his life. He would go on to shoot an 80, his lowest score ever.

As we approached the tenth tee, I asked McLean to team up with me for the second nine. It was agreed that he would get two strokes a hole. He had just shot 69 on the front, and it seemed unlikely that he would make much of a contribution, but I was ready to try anything to stop the bleeding, and Paul and Brian were feeling annoyingly invincible.

McLean responded like a champion. He shot a 60 on the back, his lowest score to date by several shots. His clutch seven (reduced by his two-shot handicap to a five) on the eighteenth hole preserved our one-up victory on the back, and though I had lost the front and the eighteen, his stellar performance made it feel as if we'd taken it all.

A little miracle had taken place right before my eyes. For this journey over nine holes, McLean forsook his solitary journey and became one of the guys. He watched what all of us were doing, keeping track of all our shots, knowing what he needed to do to make a contribution to our team. Everything about him—the way he walked, the care he took over each shot—indicated determination. Doubtless, he wanted to be on the winning team, but it was just as clear that he delighted at his inclusion in our game.

There was just a single moment that morning that McLean stood out as the child in our midst. We were walking down the fourth fairway when he called over to me.

"I have a pretty bad stomachache, Dad," he said, his expression pained.

This gastrointestinal discomfort came as no surprise to me. When he was home, his diet was primarily vegetarian. At his grandmother and grandfather's house, he had been eagerly consuming an average of two to three hot dogs a day.

"It will go away," I told him, praying that it would. I didn't expect to encounter a restroom out there, and we were miles away from the clubhouse. Fortunately it did seem to pass quickly.

Later that night, when we were reminiscing about the day, Brian recalled that moment. He admitted that he had thought to himself, in all seriousness, *I hope this kid doesn't think we're going to stop playing to take care of his tummyache.* We both laughed. "Maybe you should have encouraged him to go back to the clubhouse," I told Brian. "You would have won yourself another five bucks on the match if it wasn't for him."

McLean's golf game had been transformed that morning at Swansea Country Club. It had been forever improved, if not dramatically—it would be weeks before he broke 60—then at least permanently. His confidence had been boosted, and he had been taken to another level of the game's highs, discovering that devising a strategy for play gives golf a greater sense of reward.

I also believe that genuine magic touched my son and lifted his game that day. It was the magic of a four-some, the magic of good relationships and good teams of people working and playing together. I have always believed that we discover the outer limits of our power as people when we link up with others, giving a little and getting back a lot. I think there are many men who, on the golf course, experience friendship and extend trust and goodwill in a way more pure and full of grace than in any other area of their lives. And, whether they are aware of it or not, this is a large part of the reason they feel the need to return again and again for more.

I wanted my sons to go back for more. That's why I was so determined to put together a foursome when we got back to Rhode Island again at the end of the season.

✻

On something of a whim at the start of the summer, my father had decided to rent a big house on the ocean in the town of Narragansett, Rhode Island. He booked it for the last week in August, just before Labor Day weekend, eager to gather all his children and grandchildren under one roof. He'd always been a generous soul, and as he aged, he was becoming more and more sentimental. But the arrangement of his children's schedules wasn't as effortless as his kindness. Karen and I planned to be there with Colin and McLean from Tuesday to Saturday morning. Paul could be there only for the weekends before and after we arrived. Brian would be flying in Thursday night. Kathryn, my lone sister, older than me by a year, and Michael, a year younger than I, and their kids would be staying for the entire time. My mother and father, not really beach-goers, would make guest appearances.

Leaving for Rhode Island, I wedged three sets of golf clubs between towels and boogie boards and snorkels and fins in the back of our station wagon, trusting that we would somehow manage to work in some family golf, having won Karen's assurance that she wouldn't mind if I left her for a morning or afternoon. Under normal circumstances it wouldn't have been necessary to check with her, but there had been nothing normal about Karen's summer. She'd been experiencing the pregnancy from hell. The first two months she had morning, noon, and night sickness. Soon afterward the migraines arrived. She couldn't take medication, for it might affect the baby. She'd never had migraines before, would become weak in the knees, and she liked having me around to keep her propped up. A few weeks earlier, my sister Kathryn, her husband Jimmy, and their daughter Sara had come for their annual August visit to Saratoga and a day at the horse races. At the end of the fourth race, Karen felt the pounding begin. We were almost back to the car when she fainted. I was able to lean her against a fence until she was revived enough to keep going. We both felt chastened by the experience, realizing that we had attempted too much. If she had a bad week at the beach, I wouldn't be playing any golf.

*

Still tired after the plane trip in from Washington, D.C., the night before, Brian was slow to respond when I shook him awake at 9 A.M. on that Friday morning before the start of Labor Day weekend. I'd waited about as long as I could.

"We tee off at Jamestown Golf Course in an hour," I told him. The night before, we didn't know if it would be possible to play. I had risen early to make the arrangements.

Brian groaned and rolled over. "What about clubs?" he asked.

"They'll rent you a set," I answered. "I already called. They said getting off this morning won't be a problem. So rise and shine and give God your glory."

He groaned again.

We'd been having a wonderful vacation at the beach, Colin teaching himself to surf, McLean enjoying the company of his cousins, and Karen and I taking the opportunity to relax and read detective novels. But I figured I could push things a little and have a golfing experience, too.

Karen awoke early with me that morning, and by 6:30 we were having coffee together on the front porch of the rented beach house. The town was silent. We could see the ocean at the end of our road and hear the distant crashing of the surf.

When I was a young teenager in the mid-1960s, the seaside town of Narragansett was something of an East Coast version of a Brian Wilson fantasy. Numerous surf-board shops lined its streets, and bronzed, long-haired men and women roamed everywhere. But in the thirty years since I'd spent any time there, Narragansett had undergone a radical transformation. The main part of town, which stood directly adjacent to the beach and was once sloppy home to all the surfing safarians, had been bulldozed over and replaced with a condominium com-plex, complete with upscale shops and a movie theater. Initially I mourned the passing of the once exotic locale, but now I appreciated the proximity of this much more genteel civilization. It had taken just a short walk over to find us good coffee and muffins. We were very happy there with our coffee, listening to the surf, up well before the nine o'clock stampede of children. We could feel like real adults, relaxed, in control of our lives, smart enough to know that a day's first hours are often its best.

"The waves sound big today," I said.

"They'll wait for you," Karen answered. "Go ahead and play golf. I feel pretty good this morning."

"You're sure?"

"I'm sure," Karen insisted. "Just don't forget your hat."

I put my hand up to my head, where a bald spot had been growing for years. The day before, at the beach, I'd left my hat off for an hour, and the top of my head still glowed.

"It hurts to look at it," Karen said.

I nodded.

"I'll go find my hat now," I said. "I'm going to start taking very good care of my scalp."

"No, you're going to take very good care of your wife first," Karen said. "Let's go for a quick walk on the beach now. You've got to let Brian and the boys sleep a little longer anyway. They'd shoot you if you tried to get them up now.

"And one more thing," Karen said, as we finished off our coffee and stood to go out. "Play well today, will you? I can't stand any more whining."

*

I had never played the Jamestown Golf Course, though I had driven past it many times in my youth en route to Newport. Jamestown is an island wedged in between the Rhode Island mainland and Newport, its popular tourist destination. Newport still has magnificent mansions from the days when it was the most exclusive resort community in America, and is home to the Newport Country Club, the site of the first United States Open and Amateur golf championships. Jamestown is a peaceful and unassuming island, offering views from its craggy coastline of distant seas. Many of its rolling green hillsides are squared off with old stone walls.

Though separated from Newport Country Club by just a narrow strip of water, and though it, too, was opened in 1895, making it one of the first public golf courses in America, Jamestown Golf Course has no proud pedigree of which it can boast. I have no doubt, however, that many a golfer who has played there over the last hundred years has had himself a very special time.

The day we played the course came at the end of this very dry summer, and though the fairways were baked to a crusty brown, the greens had been sufficiently watered to keep them quite lush. The knowledge that it had been there for over a century made the Jamestown course our own little Rhode Island version of St. Andrews.

In other words, we all played very well that day, and sometimes, when we play so well, poetic license is taken when serving up our memories.

Colin gave notice on the first hole that he had come to play, knocking his third shot, a full nine-iron, to within four feet of the hole. He was teamed up with Brian to take on McLean and me. And though he missed his par putt, with a two-stroke handicap on the hole, Colin's net three was good enough for the win. He continued to play with increasing consistency, and were it not for a disastrous nine on the eighth hole could have shot much better than his final 61.

He and Brian were a tough team. We were all even after five holes, though I had put together a string of five pars. McLean's play was desultory, and I had to take him aside after the third hole and admonish him to quit with his pouting. "Sure, a seven, nine, eight start stinks," I said, "but we've got six holes to go, and I need you in this with me." McLean glowered but went on to answer the call, playing the next six holes very well and finishing with his best score to date, a 58.

Our match was all even coming to the ninth hole, a 326-yard par four. With the hard fairways, I had visions of driving the green, and almost did. I was fifteen yards short and to the right. But the others were playing the hole just as well. Brian, getting a stroke here, put his second shot to within fifteen feet. Colin was on in five and McLean in four, each of them receiving two strokes on the hole.

In the end, Brian's four, net three, won the hole and the match. But not until Colin had made a strong run at his putt and McLean had grazed the cup in his bid for a net birdie. My routine par, though it brought me in at a happy 39, was inconsequential.

What was of consequence, I would realize in retrospect, was the great fun Colin had had, his enthusiasm for golf never before so apparent, and the lesson McLean had learned in not giving up. When school started the following week, Colin signed up for the golf club and began playing Monday afternoons. From then on, whenever McLean played poorly, I would remind him about his turnaround at Jamestown, and though he might not always show it, he would not give up again so easily.

So, each in our own ways, the three of us had discovered that while golf may be a contest against the self, many of its blessings are received in the communion of others. In the company of friends and family we are blessed with a certain lightness of being that makes our trials less burdensome and our spirits more able to soar.

Or maybe it was only I who had made this discovery. Colin and McLean were having pleasurable experiences, their play was improving, and their appreciation of the game had been enhanced. But I was still doing the conducting. It might be that this entire adventure really mattered only to me, and my sons were humoring me. My intention certainly wasn't to have them learn how to live the dreams I might have for their lives. They needed to discover how to create and meet the demands of their own great expectations.

How do we figure out what matters to us, and then go about successfully pursuing our goals? That lesson lay before us.

To play well you must feel tranquil and at peace. I have never been troubled by nerves in golf because I felt I had nothing to lose and everything to gain.

—HARRY VARDON
✲

6

✤

IN THE GROOVE

Sometimes comprehension comes to us only after what we have been staring at is removed from our view, and in its absence we understand just what it was that had been sitting directly in front of us. Now that we see it so clearly, we can't believe we were so shortsighted as to not know it all along. And in this new awareness, of course, we want this object of our attention to be returned to us forthwith, so that we might appreciate it at last in its fullness.

Sometimes, if we are lucky, we are granted this opportunity, but more often, we can't simply command the return of things that we had not fully grasped or appreciated. We must endure a period of purgatory during which, no matter how sincere our feelings or the passion of our pleading, we suffer a terrible longing.

That's how it was with my own golf game the season I taught my sons to play. I myself acquired a profound appreciation for what it means to play "in the groove," that is, to play well while experiencing a joyful calm. But I gained that knowledge only after my ability to play in this manner had left me. And despite my best efforts to apply what I had learned and begin to play well again immediately, I could not.

However frustrated this experience left me, I remained confident that once my time in purgatory had been served I would rise up again one day soon. And I felt confident, too, that I could share what I had come to understand about getting in the groove with my sons.

*

Many are inclined to view playing in the groove as existing in something like a state of grace. There do seem to be similarities. As I understand the theologian's exploration of the subject, God bestows his graces upon us when and how he sees fit, and we should not ever expect to fully understand his logic. However—and this is a very significant however—we *can* increase our chances of receiving grace. We can, by our behavior, position ourselves in a good spot. We can be charitable, we can be pure of heart, we can be thankful for what we do have and not be dispirited by what we lack. And when we have met these requirements, though we should not for a moment think that we are owed God's lightning in a bottle, we might dare hope that we have become a candidate for grace.

Carrying this paradigm over to golf, we would say that we should do our practicing conscientously, free ourselves of the day's distractions in order to be entirely in the moment when we play, and, most important of all, leave it up to the golfing gods as to whether we get to play in the groove on a particular round.

But while I think this attitude can at times serve us admirably, it is a much too passive approach to take as a consistent model of behavior. There *are* actions we can take, there is a way of thinking and behaving, that can put us in the groove. We can achieve it on our own. We can learn to put our own lightning in a bottle.

I have come to this conclusion after a careful examination of my many and varied experiences with golf, after puzzling over my triumphs and travails, and after peering into the mysteries of my ever-changing attitudes while playing.

When I started playing golf again in my early thirties, after ten years without so much as picking up a club, I did so at the invitation of a friend. And because I could see how much he loved to play, because I enjoyed his company, playing golf with him was simply an opportunity to have a good time.

Michael Bamberger and I were fellow reporters on the staff of the *Vineyard Gazette*, a newspaper chronicling the life and times of the island of Martha's Vineyard. He and I would play a few holes of golf on the occasional summer evening when neither of the two of us had a meeting to cover for the paper. Colin was two or three years old at the time, and because I enjoyed having him with me, I would bring him along as we played. Sometimes he walked beside me at a half-trot, holding my hand. Sometimes it became necessary to carry him between shots. When I reached my ball, I would place him down on the ground a few paces away, from where he could sit and watch, and then step up and hit my shot.

What was so pleasurable about these evenings, in addition to the time out with my son and a good friend, was how my golf game returned to me so willingly, though I had so cavalierly abandoned it a decade before. Michael, as companionable a playing partner as one could ever hope to have, told me that I played as much like a natural as anyone he had ever seen, a remark that made the experience more delightful still. Nobody had ever called me a natural at anything before, and the effect of such praise was powerful. I accepted the compliment, believed it, and acted accordingly, continuing to play as a natural would, simply stepping up to the ball, striking it, and watching it soar off in the direction of the flagstick. I was not concerned with my score, for a natural knows enough to let the score take care of itself. I was content simply to play.

I had quit golf at age twenty because I felt nothing like a natural. Back then, I would typically start off doing well, but as the round progressed and the opportunity to get under 80 beckoned, I would become frantic with a need to achieve a low score. I would calculate exactly what had to happen over the final three holes to bring me to my goal. The end, the final score, would become my total reason for being. I would walk these final three holes as if I were edging along the gangplank, staring down at the hostile water below. More often than not, I ended up soaked with disappointment.

I also stopped playing because I no longer kept the company of golfers. It had been even longer since I played with someone who took pleasure in seeing me do well, rather than openly or covertly matching their card against mine. During my final year playing golf at Warwick Country Club as a teenager, all of us had become very competitive.

These times golfing with Michael Bamberger on Martha's Vineyard were brief, but their effect was long-lasting. For the next several years I played whenever the opportunity presented itself, with a sense of amazement and gratitude that I could still play well. It gave me an incredible charge, and though I feigned an "Aw, shucks" pose, inside I was usually giddy with pleasure.

Eventually, I began to play with more regularity, and eventually my attitude changed. It didn't seem such a big deal to play well when playing regularly. That didn't make me a natural, did it?

By the time Karen and I went on our honeymoon to Ireland, I was becoming stuck again. Golf frustrated me as often as it brought me satisfaction. I knew that I would never again let a bad round get to me the way it had in my youth, but I was coming to believe that the more I played the less I could enjoy it because the more I played the more I would become fixed on achieving a low score rather than enjoying the game. But golfing in Ireland released me from this malaise. Walking the windy seaside links with Karen, I realized how completely alive I felt while playing. This experience didn't feel at all as if it had come to me as some capricious act of God. Rather, it seemed my birthright.

And yet, I could not then have articulated what it was I had discovered about golf, about myself, and about playing in the groove. I simply proceeded, over the next year, to play the best golf of my life. I can't recall a single bad round. I was under 80 several times, and rarely shot more than 85, while never practicing or playing with any great regularity. My father would joke with me about starting to get ready for the Senior Tour, and for a flickering moment I would indulge myself in the fantasy.

Then, during the weeks leading up to the time I started to teach Colin and McLean to play, I became a voracious reader of golf books. Intellectually, I began to examine the game in all its details and nuances. As I watched the pros on television, I carefully studied their swings, and their various preshot routines.

When we got out to play that summer, I immediately began to tinker. The previous season I had settled into playing the ball with a slight fade, but I wanted now to hit the ball as I had during boyhood, with a draw. Later, I brought home a video camera from the office, under the pretense of showing the boys their swings, when actually I wanted to have a look at what my own swing looked like. Running the tape again and again, I was horrified by what I saw. My swing wasn't a classic. My backswing was too short. My stance was too wide. I began to tinker further.

That summer and fall I didn't break 80 once. There were many rounds in the high 80s, and even a couple in the nineties. Eventually I would abandon the draw, the narrower stance, and the longer backswing. I would beg forgiveness from the golfing gods, promising never again to abuse my gifts. But it was all to no avail: Golfing had become difficult. I was way out of the groove.

✳

It was early in September, after I finally decided to give up on my game, for this year at least, that the boys and I discovered the Pioneer Hills public golf course. I had seen the ad in the newspaper earlier in the summer announcing its opening, and it was just fifteen miles away, but we had never gotten around to playing there. I had decided the Saratoga Spa course was our home track, and that golfing there regularly could provide a consistent benchmark of our progress.

But as the days grew shorter and we needed to get out on the course earlier in the afternoon in order to complete our rounds, we were finding the Spa course a little too crowded for our tastes. The Spa course, I would soon learn, had also become too much associated with benchmarks and progress.

Pioneer Hills provided much more than a change of scenery: It gave me a great big shift in view.

In order to help Colin and McLean achieve a body-mind connection, it had been necessary for a time to curtail their natural sense of playfulness. They had needed discipline, for they had insufficient respect for control and consistency. But I realized on the very first afternoon we played Pioneer Hills that we could all benefit from another injection of joy. If the boys could learn to combine their playfulness with their recently acquired due diligence, they could get in the groove.

I came to my big shift in point of view in part because Pioneer Hills was so short. At just 2,515 yards, this nine-hole, par-thirty-five layout made me feel like a world beater, or, more to the point, like a natural. I could hit irons off the tee and still hit the par fours with very short irons.

Just as significant, I noticed that, in its infancy, this was a delicately pretty course. There was a homemade quality about the place, as if it had been designed by someone like me who had always dreamed of buying some land and hopping on the bulldozer. It featured nothing fancy—just narrow swaths through the woods, with water coming into play on a couple of holes, and a few elevated tees and sharp doglegs. For a course that had been open only a few months, it was remarkably lush. The greens were in great shape, and the putts rolled true.

Colin and McLean also liked the fact that Pioneer Hills was short, and that it had no sand traps. You could feel like lord of the manor at such a place.

With school back in session and their lives getting busier, more often than not I was playing with either Colin or McLean alone. This, too, proved fortuitous, for now they weren't distracted by the need to compete with each other. We walked along as partners playing this friendly little course. And because word apparently hadn't spread about Pioneer Hills, and because we usually played late on a Saturday or Sunday, we usually went around without ever being held up. It seemed as if it was our very own course, on which we had stepped outside of normal time and space. I felt calm and carefree. And in this calm all my senses clicked on. The grass seemed very green for this time of year. The breezes freshened. I noticed, too, how these breezes tinkled the leaves on the trees as if they were little bells. I had found again what it means to be in the groove.

Usually we come to this experience only by stumbling into it. The conditions are there: We're playing with someone whose company we enjoy, we're just happy to be out, we notice and appreciate the beauty of nature, we're not fixed on outcomes and expectations, and, lo and behold, we have one of those days when we play like a wizard.

But the real key is that we have an experience that's not about *doing* anything. Rather, it's about *being*. It's about feeling alive. Our senses are entirely awake.

When I was a boy playing golf at Warwick Country Club, we would often go out onto the course very early. I can vividly recall the roll of the ball making lines across the green, shooting out a little fantail of dew as it made its silent journey to the hole. The world was redolent of the freshly cut grass piled near the back corners of the greens. As we stood on the ninth tee alongside Narragansett Bay, I would watch the fishing boats fight their way through the chop as I considered how the strength of the wind would affect the flight of my ball.

Such a heightening of my senses is not a part of my everyday life. I tend to live entirely in my mind. Nearly every experience I have is immediately filtered through my preconceived notions about what's good or bad, beautiful or ugly, worth doing or not. I've never been very spontaneous. Quite literally, I have never been one to

153

stop and smell the roses—except on the golf course, where I seem naturally inclined to appreciate the flowers and the trees, and the careful cut of the grass. I can't help but proclaim at least once a round how lucky I am to be doing what I'm doing, seeing what I see, smelling what I smell, playing with a pal.

Colin and McLean inevitably chuckle at these proclamations, accustomed as they are to thinking their father has a tendency to get a little goofy.

I noticed, too, during that fall's games at Pioneer Hills that Colin and McLean also had their own more private reactions to my unabashed expressions of appreciation. McLean would display a little embarrassment, overwhelmed, I believe, by his similar reaction of thanks when things were going well, and by how this made him aware of his emotions. Colin would seem to puff out his chest, ready to take credit for knowing how to have a good time.

"It just doesn't get any better than this, does it?" I asked one Saturday afternoon as the three of us approached the sixth hole at Pioneer Hills, a very short par three with an elevated tee and a small green surrounded by marsh.

"It's because you're playing well, Dad," Colin explained.

"So you noticed," I said.

"Well, you haven't played well in a long time," McLean added.

"So you noticed that, too," I replied, smiling.

"You've been moaning about it enough," Colin remarked, looking away from me toward the green. He tugged on his baseball cap, pulling it down on his forehead.

"I don't moan," I said. "Just for the record, I cry out in anguish."

"Whatever," Colin answered. He pulled a club from his bag and walked out onto the tee.

"Watch that swampy area to the left, hotshot," I told him.

"Watch me put this right up close to the pin," Colin said.

"Feeling good about this hole, are you?"

"This hole is just like our ninth hole," he replied. "I've got this hole covered."

"Our ninth hole" is the little golf hole we had constructed on our property earlier in the summer. What a time we'd had with it. It began as a great reclamation project the previous summer. A half-acre of swamp lay next to our side yard, which we imagined might easily be turned into a sweet little pond, encircled by a thick, green carpet of grass, over which Karen and I would gaze and enjoy tranquility, and on which the boys, their friends, and I would play boisterous games of hockey.

Several thousand dollars later, after months of wavering attention by the fellow with the backhoe, we had our little pond, encircled by a new swamp of mud and rocks. When the time came the following summer to rake out the rocks (which were now embedded in the crusted mud) and plant grass, there was drought. We planted anyway, and, after weeks of pulling hoses and positioning and repositioning sprinklers, we produced vast stretches of brown stubble.

Somewhere in the middle of this madness, I had a vision: We would put a golf tee on one side of the pond, a small green on the other, and create a scenic water hole all our own, where we would sponsor tournaments by special invitation.

My vision took form only reluctantly. After failing in the effort to grow grass, I bought a six-foot-square section of sod for our tee and managed to get it to take root, though it never got much past a greenish brown. To make our green, I planted a fifteen-foot circle of bent grass, but as I neglected to follow the rather rigorous requirements for the proper planting of this type of seed, I had another laughable result. The boys and I finally settled for a blue plastic drinking cup burrowed down into a "somewhat grassy" area. Into this cup we stuck a ten-foot length of pvc pipe hung with a patch of light blue cloth bearing a dark blue numeral "9"—this "9," of course, being in honor of the ninth hole at Warwick Country Club, the water hole of my golfing youth.

It was Colin who really brought our ninth hole to life. While my grand scheme to create a world-class tee box and putting green fizzled, Colin set out to make a simple wood sign to place next to the tee and created a work of art. He found a scrap piece of two-by-six and sanded it smooth. In slate blue, he painted the numeral "9," as well as the length of the hole, "60 yards." Then he added a picture of a small white golf ball, up on a tee, surrounded by tufts of green grass. Finally, he painted a small portrait of the hole, as seen from the perspective of the hawks that often circle overhead. The sign complete, he then went about finding two round rocks and painted them bright white, making them tee markers.

We dragged over a bench from another part of the property to sit behind the tee, and it, the white markers, and the sign, now attached to a length of thick branch cut from a nearby tree and banged securely into the ground, produced a vision far different but no less lovely than my original concept.

That ninth hole was perfect for us at our station at the beginning of golfing life. The boys were then content to make contact with the ball, and to send one sailing over that sixty-yard expanse of water was a daunting prospect. Dozens and dozens of old golf balls plunked into the murky depths, and despite Colin and McLean's best efforts with snorkels and fins, we were never able to re-cycle these miscues.

But many a summer evening we fought off the mos-quitoes and played that hole. The sand wedge got to be the most accurate club in my bag. The boys went from first swinging away at their drivers, doing anything they could to make the distance, entirely unconcerned about where the ball might end up, to eventually hitting their seven-irons across the water with some degree of accu-racy.

Mostly I remember that we had fun. It was like it had been for me as a boy throwing a baseball around on summer evenings after dinner with the other kids in the neighborhood. I would take my position across the pond behind the pale blue flag, and if Colin or McLean man-aged to hit one over safely, I would retrieve it and heave it back over for them to hit again. For a time, we tried the floating golf balls that are sold in some golf shops, but these floaters would linger out in the center of the pond for days before eventually making their way to shore, which proved more annoying than watching the real balls disappear instantly. And besides, the floaters took the terror out of the game, and it was the terror that so thrilled the boys in the early days of our golfing adventure.

✻

So, as Colin stood at the sixth hole at Pioneer Hills that afternoon, he drew confidence from feeling he knew the shot. He had, however, failed to note the yardage. Though entirely downhill, the distance was at least a club longer than our ninth hole. His seven-iron was right on line, but five yards short of the green.

"Nice shot," I told him.

He smiled. He knew he had hit it well. "I can still get a par," he said.

"Yes, you can," I agreed. And he almost did. He made a pretty good chip, about ten feet short of the hole, but missed the putt. Four was a nice score, however, and he was happy with it.

"You're in the groove now, buddy," I said.

Colin chuckled. It was the first time I had used that

expression. "Yeah," he said, strutting toward the next tee and snapping his fingers to some imaginary beat. "I'm in the groove, man."

He'd made a joke of it, but in that moment, in the company of his father and brother, calling upon his experiences at our own ninth hole, where we'd created something special out of nothing and had a lot of laughs doing so, he had indeed put himself in the groove.

An unabashed enjoyment of golf sets the stage for excellence. Most of us realize that if we tense up and try too hard while playing, if we overanalyze or overthink, the consequences are as severe as when we let our attention shift away. But what we may not understand is that as we let the furrows in our brow deepen, we lose our sense of play, and that this is precisely the problem. There is tension and conflict where there needs to be eagerness. And without this essential ingredient of childlike eagerness our actions become mechanized and lifeless. There is no groove. To be truly in the groove is to have an internal awareness that is repeatable at will. The work of the will is to let go.

Most of us have the experience of being in the groove in snatches of time, during stretches of holes when the ball flies straight and true, and the putts drop.

We should learn to revel in these moments, milking them for every last ounce of their exquisite pleasure.

We've all watched the great players go on hot streaks, winning a major tournament or maybe even two, only to suddenly lose whatever it was that lifted them on high. We are told that these great players have become distracted by new opportunities, drained by the increased attention lavished on them by their fans. It is said, too, that they have lost the fire that once burned brightly and fueled their desire to achieve greatness. Certainly there is some validity to these postulations. But we know, by instinct and our own experiences with the game, that these explanations do not really satisfy. We have felt our own championship moments, however we modestly define them, leave us, even though we are presented no endorsement contracts and are not entreated to sit for interview sessions.

All of us get out of the groove because we fail to notice how we get into the groove in the first place.

Human beings, most all of us, are inherently hopeful. But too often our hopefulness is undercut by a feeling of desperation. Because we don't take the time to examine in detail what exactly contributes to the making of our successes, they remain a mystery to us, and out of our control. But once we make that examination, we will find that there are particular steps we can take, certain circumstances that are more favorable, specific attitudes that we can adopt that will give us the experience we seek. Being in the groove isn't a state of grace, it is a state of mind. Being in a state of grace is a gift from God to us. Being in the groove is our gift to God in return, our celebration of the fact that we're embracing all the opportunities laid before us.

There is in fact a formula for getting in the groove, and it was revealed to me that season I taught my sons to play golf.

We begin with a sense of play, a sense of pleasure in whatever activity we are engaged in. Through trial and adjustment, we then create a solid mind-body connection. We practice this activity, through a disciplined effort, until we have repeated it enough to make it a body memory. Then, through appreciation, we learn to pay attention and be in the moment. This gives us an unparalleled feeling of oneness, with no separation between our play, our skill, or our sense of appreciation.

When we're playing in the groove, we aren't *doing* anything. Because no effortful thought process is involved, we experience an intuition that is as infallible as it is joyful, and we have unquestioning faith in our ability to achieve the results we desire. All the senses have come into play. We feel so alive that we don't have the time or inclination to consider anything other than how good it is to be alive.

In my lifetime there is one golfing champion who stands out among all the rest, and who has sustained his greatness well beyond winning a major championship or two. I should not have been surprised to find that in reading Jack Nicklaus's thoughts on golf I would find a clear explanation of what has kept him in the groove over all these years.

"I began to play the game because I liked it," he says in the book he wrote with Ken Bowden, *Jack Nicklaus, On and Off the Fairway*, "and I've gone on playing simply because I love it. It may not sound convincing to people when I say that money and applause have always been incidental, but that's the truth. Neither have ever motivated me to try harder or play better. What has is just the sheer challenge of the game itself, of doing something as well as I possibly can, purely for the enjoyment of that effort and the personal satisfaction I enjoy when I am successful. I happen to believe that most high-achievers have the same motivation. I also happen to believe that when they lose it, or begin to put the rewards ahead of the fun of doing one's best for its own sake, is when they begin to fail."

It is this knowledge, the adoption of this approach to every challenge we face, that I desired for myself, and for my sons.

My father rarely offered me advice without
an invitation, but when I did ask for his
thoughts I listened to them carefully because
he was extremely knowledgeable about all
aspects of the game.

—JACK NICKLAUS
✽

7

*

TEACHING OUR CHILDREN WELL

Upon first learning that *Harvey Penick's Little Red Book* was one of the most popular sports books of all time, I was incredulous. If asked to speculate on the genre's greatest hits, I would have rattled off titles bearing the names of famous athletes with real star power. I dare say I wouldn't have even figured Mr. Penick for the top twenty. But in fact, at that point I hadn't yet read *Harvey Penick's Little Red Book*. I think it's also instructive to point out that I came of age in the 1960s, a time when youth led a wild charge away from the wisdom of the elders. Such ignorance will inevitably leave a residue.

Now that I have finally joined the ranks of its millions of readers I have little difficulty understanding what made Mr. Penick's book so popular. It bears its author's witness to an eloquent kindness, which should serve as a heartening example to people everywhere. Fundamentally, it's about helping us to be ourselves, which is, after all, our preferred way of realizing our goals, and it represents the accumulated wisdom of an individual who spent decades in selfless consideration of how good golf might be made accessible to others—which means that golfers can expect to find in Mr. Penick's ruminations practical, understandable solutions to their problems.

Golfers require only modest expectation of insight, because they thirst for it so. Take the great Bobby Jones, who was as smart about golf as he was talented. He once remarked that this was the one game he knew that became more and more difficult the more one played. He speculated that it was precisely this endless opportunity for refining one's skills and trying to improve that might be golf's greatest allure. This desire to be better not only leads to a thirst for knowledge, it also promotes an abiding respect for teachers. We shouldn't be surprised, then, to learn that word among golfers had spread far and wide about Harvey Penick long before his book pushed him into the spotlight.

Most golfers realize that others can see more clearly and objectively than they can themselves what they're doing wrong. Even those who in all other areas of their lives insist on knowing it all will humbly accept advice from a fellow golfer, especially in times of need. In life we are inclined to protest, "You don't know what I'm going through. You can't possibly understand." In golf, however, when we say to a person, "I've been there," that person usually acknowledges that we have.

That's why, on a golf course, I am far more likely to offer unsolicited advice than I am in almost every other arena of life. You can tell most golfers that they have started swinging too hard, or that they are dipping into the ball, and they will probably be grateful. This is not the case when commenting uninvited on someone's marital or financial problems.

For many years now I have operated, as best as I can, under the dictum that advice to others about their personal affairs should be offered only upon request. But with my children, I believe that I have been charged with the responsibility of teaching them all I can about life, liberty, and the pursuit of happiness, and that I should fearlessly push my opinions on them, whether they like it or not.

The authoritarian posture did not come naturally to me. Until that summer when I taught Colin and McLean to play golf, and began actively to instruct them in matters of integrity, responsibility, and love, I was like that teacher everybody loved in high school, that one who was easy to talk to, didn't worry much about missed homework assignments, and was just trying to make it all as interesting as he possibly could. He was a great guy, though we can't quite remember whether we got much out of his class.

I have already explained how the more involved stance I took in schooling my sons in the areas of character and values came after conversations I had had with them about cheating, and the rather blasé reaction they had to the episode of "Golf, the Great Game of Honor." But I had also been influenced in this regard by an encounter I'd had with my own father several years earlier, a few nights after he learned over the phone that Colin and McLean's mother and I were separating.

My father had insisted that we meet for a discussion immediately, at some point between Rhode Island and Saratoga. While failed marriages may be commonplace today, for my parents this was news tantamount to that of a death. My father wanted assurance, face to face, that before pulling the plug I had done everything in my power to keep the marriage alive.

On the drive to Springfield, Massachusetts, to meet with him that night I was both distraught and profoundly nervous. As well as discussing the difficulties of my marriage, I felt I needed to talk with my father about my relationship with him. I wanted to come clean about everything. For years I had wanted to know him more completely, had wanted to tell him that I'd always felt anxious for his love and approval. I knew he loved me, but I wanted him to show it more explicitly—say, in the way he might confide in me about his personal affairs, or in the way he might eagerly draw from me all the details of my emotional life. It seemed we had such conversations only in moments like these, when tragedy struck.

He was wearing blue jeans that night. I remember that detail because as emotionally overwrought as I was, when I first spotted him in the restaurant lobby I couldn't help but smile. I'd never seen him in jeans, for he had always been a shirt-and-tie guy. When I was a kid, he would come home at the end of the day in his business clothes and sit right down to eat with us. The night would go on, and my last image was of him dozing off in front of the television, the tie still neatly positioned under his chin. Yet there was nothing starchy about him, as he wore his uniform of a pinstriped blue buttoned-down cotton shirt with a black Irish knit tie quite comfortably. And now he was in blue jeans and looking comfortable still. He had said he was thoroughly enjoying his recent retirement, and I could observe the results for myself.

In his image I could also see myself as I would look in twenty-five years, because I had been told often enough that I resembled him more and more as I aged. My eyes would still be a bright blue, but I would have only a scattering of graying hair on the top of my head. My fair Irish skin would be liberally dappled in browns and reds from too much time exposed to the sun. I would appear lean, but deceptively so. At five feet ten and a half inches tall, exactly my height, my father probably weighed a solid 170 pounds. But the long face was the face of a thin man. If I would appear as distinguished, and as warm and friendly as he now did, I considered, I would be pleased.

In addition to an evolving physical likeness, my life had also, quite unwittingly, followed closely that of my father in the ways we displayed our talents and provided for our families. He had started out as a newspaper reporter and written columns, before switching to the advertising business, and finally joining in partnership to run an advertising and public relations company. So had I. I say "unwittingly" because when I was a boy I had little idea or interest in what my father did all day, and it never once occurred to me to pursue a job at a newspaper. As a young man the only time I gave much thought to my father's work in advertising was when this field was portrayed during my college years as full of evil manipulators. Never in my wildest dreams would I have placed myself among them. But when the time came to get a job and pursue a career, I realized I had inherited his writing skill. It took me, naturally enough, though without any formal plan, to newspapers, and then to advertising. I was, after all, my father's son.

My father opened the conversation that night immediately after the waitress took our dinner order. "I was thinking about my father today," he began, looking directly across the table at me, "as I was thinking about coming here to meet you. My father died when I was overseas during the war . . . I was thinking that I can't recall anything that my father and I did together. Or talked about. I can't remember any treasured moments. Or a feeling of closeness. There are times when I still feel a lingering sadness and emptiness. I wonder sometimes whether there was a time and place that slipped by us when something special could have happened."

He stopped, looked away, and then back to me.

"I guess what I'm trying to tell you is that I never really learned how a father talks to a son."

My eyes filled. I shook my head, unable to speak. In that moment, by simply acknowledging that these conversations did not come easily to him, that this simply wasn't his way, he flattened the little neurotic demons that had been dancing in my head for so many years.

After I had composed myself, I told him everything. I told him I'd been worrying for a long time that I'd been a disappointment to him, that I knew my emotional needs had sometimes overwhelmed him, and that even though I had let my life go off on more than a few wild tangents I really did have my eye on the ball. I had never lost the desire to build a successful career, to be a good father and provider, and to make a lasting contribution to the world.

Upon the conclusion of my choked-up and at times incoherent confession, my father smiled. "I never doubted for a minute that you would realize your dreams," he said.

"Yes, you did," I insisted. "You thought I was full of shit."

"I didn't say that there weren't times when I thought you were off the beam," he admitted.

I nodded.

"But what bothers me is that you even doubted whether you had my approval," he continued, earnestly. "You always had my approval, in the sense that I have always loved you, and I always believed that eventually you would get it right. For example, you know that I didn't agree with your decision to move to Martha's Vineyard. I didn't think it made sense for you and your career at that time in your life. But then when I saw the quality of the work you did there, I was very impressed with it. I remember writing and telling you that."

I nodded again, and then a door was unlocked that let me step back in time. I saw my sister Kathy, brother Michael, and myself as young children. I might have been five then, which would make Kathy six and Michael four. We were with my father at Roger Williams State Park. Because he was working nights at the newspaper, he would often take us during the day to the park, where we would toss breadcrumbs to the ducks or go rolling down the hillsides through the leaves. Few children spent as much time with their fathers, I recognized now, because few fathers so happily seized the opportunity.

As I returned to the moment at hand, I heard my father begin speaking again.

"You weren't always eager to listen to my opinions," he reminded me.

He was right. Like many of my age, I'd come home from college with hair down to my shoulders, and a reliably combative attitude about nearly everything. I spouted tirades of generalities absorbed at protest rallies: My father's generation had sold out to capitalism, and it had been left to my generation to recapture the moral high ground, to stop the war and save the planet.

For the most part, my father suffered these diatribes in silence, except for those times when I upset my mother, whereupon he would motion me into another room and, in controlled fury, remind me that it was my parent's toil and considerable sacrifice that provided me the opportunity to go off to college and have my mind filled with such theories. He would remind me, too, that it was, at the very least, rude to blithely accept someone's food and shelter while disparaging the manner by which they had come by these accommodations.

On those infrequent occasions when my father had displayed anger, I immediately went into shock, because he was so obviously a mild-mannered fellow, and I would be remorseful for weeks. But because I was spending far too much time tuned into the messages of what was then called the counterculture, it was at least once a year during the decade of my twenties that my father felt compelled to give me a strong dose of his reality, hoping, I suppose, that eventually it would become a reality we could share.

My father would have to wait until I was well into my thirties before we openly agreed on nearly all the same ideas as to what goes into the making of a good world, as well as a good life. I have always appreciated how he never took the opportunity to ridicule me for those many years I spent tilting at windmills, complaining more than working, and refusing to recognize that wisdom does come with experience. He was just relieved that I finally found security and happiness, and had hardly cared how I found it. That was always my hang-up. I wished to appear sensitive and creative even as I accumulated my fortune.

I was very much a product of my times. In all the reflecting I've done about the generation of the sixties I return again and again to its central and most devastating conceit—we thought we knew so much more than our elders. Youth is by nature inclined, for a time, to rebel, to make a run against the established mores, to disparage the accomplishments of the adults. We, however, turned it into a shared national obsession. It was as if anyone over thirty deserved to be brought up on charges for the crime of having lived a cautious life. The great tragedy is that we cut ourselves off from wisdom. Without teachers, we wandered far longer in the wilderness than was necessary.

I know that I didn't make it easy for my father to reach me. I know, too, that my father and I never suffered for lack of mutual love. It was never a lack of respect on my part, either. I had always admired my father, for his kindness and for the incontestable strength of his work ethic. What I hadn't realized was that both these qualities were, in fact, expressions of his love. Sitting there in Springfield that night, it was all revealed to me. For the men of his generation, reared in the Depression and then sent across the ocean to fight in the Second World War, simply providing for a family, and being able to give to others in this way, was a great and honorable act of love.

We, their children, benefactors of their labor, grew up in a time of plenty. We had the luxury of considering much more than where our next meal might come from. Many of us spent considerable time talking about love openly, while exploring and expressing our emotions. And we came to experience the relative silence of our fathers in these areas as disapproval or anger. What was in fact largely a generational difference, we took personally. It was when I finally stopped taking it personally that I began to feel a closeness with my father that has continued to grow over time. I very much wish that I got this process started at an earlier age.

So, when it became apparent that, in the rearing of my own sons I had been practicing a form of benign neglect, that I was operating under a number of questionable assumptions about what my sons understood about life and about my relationship with them, it caused me to sit up straight. This, in turn, caused Colin and McLean to become a little startled, too. They could hardly turn around, I know it often seemed to them, without hearing their father launch into what they came to call, not always affectionately, "Dad's lectures."

Most often, "Dad's lectures" began clumsily. I'd get something on my mind, something would bother me about the boys' behavior, or in my travels I would have a burst of insight, and I could hardly contain myself. I was never able to wait for a germane moment when I might gently turn the discussion my way. If given the slightest opening, I would go marching forward.

There was the night that summer, for example, when the boys, Karen, and I were seated around the kitchen table, eating ice cream. Colin had mentioned that he might want one day to attend the University of Vermont, because it afforded the opportunity to ski often, and because Vermont, in his mind at least, had a certain cachet.

"Why, I thought you'd have your sights set on Skidmore," I said in mock surprise, "so you could stay right here close to home. And continue to enjoy the constant companionship of your father."

"Keep dreaming, Dad," Colin said, and then filled his mouth with the cool mint chocolate chip.

"So what does being part of a family mean to you?" I asked, putting down my spoon. "Or *does* it mean anything to you?"

"Just because I want to go to Vermont to college?" Colin snapped back.

"No, I'm just curious. How important is family to you?"

"It's important."

"Don't try to shut me up," I said.

"It's important Dad, it's important," he repeated.

"So how do you make us aware of that? Let's say, how do you make McLean and I aware of this importance you place on family?"

"Here you go again, Dad."

"Could you please answer my question?"

"I don't know, Dad."

"Let me ask this another way," I tried. "How do you think people know when they're loved? How am I supposed to know that you love me?"

"You know that I love you," he answered a little sheepishly.

"How do I know?" I pressed. "When was the last time that you told me you loved me?"

"I don't have to tell you. You know."

That gave me pause, but I pushed on.

"How do you know I love you?" I asked him.

"Because you're telling me all the time that you do," he said with an embarrassed smile.

"How about that?" I said, holding up my hands, palms open. "You know I love you because I tell you."

"Maybe I don't come right out and tell you," Colin said, covering quickly, "but I leave clues."

The conversation was interrupted by a phone call. Minutes later, when I returned to the table, Colin was talking about a tool he needed to finish some project. He asked me where I thought he might find it.

"What?" I said. "I haven't been paying attention."

"That's not very considerate, Dad, " Colin said, relishing the chance to imitate what my reaction would likely have been had the tables been turned.

"I'm still back on your treasure hunt," I said, "searching for those clues you've been leaving me about how much you love me."

Karen started to laugh, and we all joined in.

Colin might have interpreted this merriment as a response to his cleverness. Actually, Karen was easily amused by her husband's wit, and generally entertained by how often my impromptu efforts to get serious with my sons left me sputtering.

"I want to be serious about this for one more minute," I said when the laughter subsided.

"Come on, Dad," Colin said. "We just had a good laugh. Let's not spoil it."

"One simple message to you two," I replied, looking over at McLean and then back at Colin. "Clues just won't do. We're a family. Let's all do what we can to make it clear that we love one another. Okay?"

"Okay," Colin said.

"Okay, McLean?" I asked.

He looked down, his face reddening a little, and nodded.

*

There is an old adage that says, "The teacher appears when the student is ready." I don't think Colin and McLean were all that ready for the series of "lectures" they attended in our kitchen and living room that summer. But I felt I had to make them ready. In a culture that values the opinions of entertainers and sports stars to inform us about what really matters, our children are not likely to be prepared for thoughtful discussions about life. In an age when children increasingly feel the need to be perfect, they're not likely to seek counsel. So I got pushy about it, while attempting to maintain a sense of humor.

McLean certainly hadn't been ready to appreciate the teachings of Dennis Walters when I urged the boys to attend that free exhibition early in the summer. Initially, I didn't think that Colin had been ready, either. He didn't seem visibly moved by Walters's remarkable surmounting of his condition, but I discovered later that he could remember vividly the flight of Mr. Walters's ball. On a couple of later occasions he told me how he loved that graceful hook, that long slow curve from right to left that Walters executed with clubs of all sizes and descriptions. Colin wished his shots would fly with that same nice curve. In this way, at least, he had been inspired.

McLean also wasn't ready yet either to learn much from Dottie Pepper, whereas our hometown heroine had impressed Colin with her accuracy and tenacity. Colin also coveted Dottie's flashy driver and her big bag. This suggested to him that there were quite tangible rewards for achievement in this sport.

McLean's first significant teacher, I believe, was my father. After the week he spent in Rhode Island, his approach to the game was transformed. Somehow, some way, his grandfather had brought him to a deeper level of appreciation. Maybe it related to the fact that McLean and my father had a history of enjoying games together.

For years, within minutes after we arrived at my parents' home from hundreds of miles away, the two of them would be off alone, well into a serious game of gin rummy. My father, seriously good at rummy, did not believe in handing his grandchildren hollow victories. McLean stayed up nights imagining the day when he would finally win a game from his grandfather. So, when they played golf together, they may well have been slipping into a well-worn groove. For me, most exciting of all, McLean became more open to instruction, which made me comfortable in finally telling him that actually I loved his big swing and wished only to guide him toward having it serve him more consistently.

Colin's major adjustment to his playing of the game—his decision to hit an iron off many of the tees—came after playing with another teenager who successfully practiced this conservative approach. I had made the suggestion on more than one occasion, and was ignored. But Colin hadn't been ready to hear it from me. For better, though more often for worse, teenagers are quite open to learning from one of their own.

I didn't much care where Colin and McLean got their education, as it was a fundamental appreciation for learning itself that I desired most for them. I couldn't imagine anything that would make me happier than to have my sons develop a general attitude about being students of life, in the way golfers develop a specific concern about learning all they can about their games. I wanted Colin and McLean to believe that if they were ever in need of help, they could go find someone to teach them what they needed to know. I wanted them to know that they didn't have to be alone in the learning process. More to the point, they *shouldn't* be alone. It's great to be creative and independent, but self-discovery is only part of the equation. Often, what's most productive is to figure out what we don't know and have the good sense to seek out the wisdom of someone who does.

This openness to instruction is also critical in learning about love. We don't learn its lessons by osmosis. How well I know that. Had I only been moved to ask my father much earlier for help in understanding the nature of our relationship, I could have had, much earlier, the quite satisfying relationship I have with him now.

✫

When it was all said and done, I realized, all the golfing teachers I paraded before my sons were really meant for me. *I* was the one who was ready for them. Time and time again that summer and fall, for instance, I thought about Dennis Walters. Usually the example of someone who has overcome a severe physical handicap stays with me for a very brief time before I forget to be thankful for my health and resume my loud complaining about trivialities. This time, the image of the paralyzed golfer lingered, repeatedly mocking my petty grumbles.

But I didn't realize the full extent to which I had been the student in that golfing season, until one evening in early fall. Karen and I were sitting out on the back deck, looking over our pond. I noticed that the flag on our homemade flagstick had started to fray, and that the wind had made the stick itself permanently stooped. Next year we would need to make a more durable replacement.

"Have you figured out yet what this little 'ninth hole' is really all about?" Karen asked me.

"What it's *really* all about?" I answered, wondering what she might slyly be getting at.

When she didn't say anything in response, I thought for a moment and offered: "It was about having a place right here, at home, where the boys and I could play . . . so we could have fun together without having to go off somewhere. . . . And I guess it was playing out some little fantasy I had about having my own golf course."

"I think it's more than that," Karen said. "I think it's much more than that."

"Okay, I give up," I said without thinking any further. "What do you think it is?"

"I think it's been about going back home for you. I think Warwick Country Club—and let's not forget that this is a little copy of that hole at Warwick Country Club—is where you go in your mind when you think of your happy times growing up. I think this has all been about you finding your way back home."

Emotional truth sometimes has immediate access to the tear ducts. I held back the tears by taking in a long breath.

I was then struck by the realization that everyone else must have recognized this truth from the beginning. I had mentioned at the outset of the project, in something of an off-handed way, about how our golf hole would be like the ninth hole at Warwick, but then Colin had taken it upon himself to make the sign and give "our ninth hole" its quite distinct identity. Maybe it was conscious, or maybe not, but he had known enough to give me pleasure in this way, and in doing so he had completed this replication.

It also occurred to me that my father had also known that the ninth hole, the most dramatic emblem of Warwick Country Club, held special significance for me. A couple of years before, he had taken me alone into the living room of my parents' house. There on the wall hung an aerial photograph of the infamous ninth. I don't remember the story of how the photo had recently come into his hands, but I remember the excitement in my father's voice as he said, "This is going to be left to you someday. I don't think anybody else could appreciate it as much." He had never before, or since, talked about inheritance.

I looked over at Karen now.

"Nine is considered a holy number in some circles, is it not?" I said flippantly.

She smiled. "Yes, we might just say that this little golf hole is your very soul, my dear."

Karen paused, and became more serious.

"Or," she said, "at least we might say that up until now, it represents one of the best ways you've found to express your spiritual nature."

"Explain, please," I said. I had a sense of what she meant, but only an incomplete one.

"Being spiritual to me means being at peace," Karen said. "From a state of peace we can radiate everything else. Love. Gratitude. Concern for others. I think golf brings you back to your center, to who you really are. It puts you at peace. It makes you feel grateful. I see that it's also where you experience the beauty of nature. In a way it is your outdoor church. It's where you commune with God."

I turned back to look over the pond. "You may be right," I said.

"I know I'm right," she said.

At first, it struck me as rather absurd that the building of a little golf hole on the property could be considered a spiritual act, but I could see clearly now that that was indeed the case.

"I need to talk to Colin and McLean about this," I said.

"Yes, you do," Karen replied.

"I've hardly talked with them about God, or the spiritual world."

"Have you thought about how you might do that?" Karen asked.

"No, I really haven't," I said. "That's the trouble, I've never been able to figure out how I want to do it."

"You will."

"I wish I was so sure."

"I've watched you in action this summer," Karen said, turning to face me. "You've been a man on a mission. Your next mission, should you choose to accept it, and I think you will, is to introduce your children to the spiritual world. A world, by the way, where you have spent a considerable amount of time."

"You mean because I have a masters degree in religious studies?" I said in a professorial tone.

"A dead giveaway," Karen retorted, "but only one of many."

I sighed heavily. "Sometimes this business of being a good parent all seems like too much to me, like I just can't pull it off," I said. "And it's making me feel old before my time."

"Older and wiser," Karen suggested.

"I sure hope so."

Golf is for smellin' heather and cut grass and walking fast across the countryside and feeling the wind and watching the sun go down and seein' your friends hit good shots and hittin' some yerself. It's love and feelin' the splendor o' this good world.

—MICHAEL MURPHY
✳

8

✳

IN THE NAME OF THE FATHER,

SON, AND HOLY SPIRIT

Colin's fourteenth birthday fell on a Saturday in that late October, and though we had made no specific plans I'd been hoping we'd play golf together that day. So my heart sank a little when he called me the night before and told me, quite excitedly, that he had put together a bike trip with his friends. The best I could do was to arrange for us to have breakfast.

Sitting over eggs and bacon in the crowded restaurant, I was incapable of saying what I had prepared in my mind lying awake in bed the night before. I had hoped to confide that in the years immediately ahead I would fully expect Colin to endure his private agonies and would make every effort not to be overly meddlesome in these personal matters. But he should avail himself of my counsel without reservation, I would also say, because there could hardly be much that he would go through that I had not. He might find my views helpful. He would not find them righteous or judgmental. I would promise him that.

But because I was tired from being up with these thoughts for half the night, and because Colin always awoke slowly, we limited our talk over breakfast to the goodness of our food and speculation on the fun he and his friends would have taking their bicycles over hill and dale.

Later that morning I hooked up with McLean, and we decided we would golf, but only if the weather improved. The temperature never rose above forty-five, and the wind never stopped howling, and so at around three o'clock I released McLean to find his friends and whatever indoor entertainment might amuse them.

After skulking around the house for an hour or so after he left, I finally laced on my running shoes and set out to make the three-mile loop over to Saratoga Lake and then back up the straight, silent stretch of road toward home. When I ran I often carried out with me the frustrations of the day, and in the toil and sweat of strenuous exercise had them washed away. In addition to this release I had also come to expect that by increasing the supply of oxygen to my brain through running, I could finally find answers to problems that had been nagging.

The problem that day was that I still hadn't found a vehicle for talking to Colin and McLean about God, and my failure was eating away at me. I felt completely at a loss. Inadequate. There was just so much to say that I didn't know where to begin.

I grew up Catholic. I was an altar boy, entertained thoughts of the priesthood, knelt down and talked to God each and every night of my young life, and never questioned that while I would certainly do some time in purgatory, the day would come at the end of time when I would meet my maker in heaven and be reunited with all my family and friends. Then I went off to college and became very lonely, and got fixed on the suffering of the innocent around the world, and began to think that the rituals of the Catholic church were silly. During my freshman year I stopped going to church. If God existed he certainly had a lot of explaining to do about the sorry state of world affairs. If God existed he had better give me proof of the fact.

I remember sitting upstairs in the college library one Sunday afternoon during my sophomore year feeling particularly lost. I had changed my major from political science to religious studies, because I'd decided that I no

FATHERS, SONS & GOLF

longer aspired to be a lawyer and United States senator, and because I wanted it explained to me, convincingly, whether in the writings of Augustine or Confucius, how my life, and the lives of the sick and needy everywhere, represented an expression of God's love. To date, all my intellectual inquiry had gained me was more bewilderment.

Bleary from my studies, I looked up from the tomes surrounding me in the tiny cubicle, out the library window, and into the white clouds hanging in the distance. "If you exist," I said, addressing God, "give me a sign." I watched, and waited. In less than a minute, the clouds moved into the shape of a cross. Or did they? If it was a cross, it was a pretty rugged one. It probably wasn't a cross at all. My eyes left the heavens and returned to my books. I banished the supposed vision from my mind. I would walk alone, without God, for many years to come.

Having children, I was awakened to the majesty and mystery of unconditional love, and in this way I was started back on the road to God. There was no defining moment, or even a series of moments that contributed to my spiritual revival. Over time I began holding conversations with God again. At first I joked with him, saying that he must have achieved an extraordinary detachment, or sense of humor, to handle what was going on down here on the planet. Later, I took the issues of right and wrong and good and evil out of the mix, figuring that in some fashion all of this apparent madness added up to something ineffably wonderful, the way my gurgling, crying, incontinent little babies added up to a feeling of love far beyond my imagination.

This tortuous personal struggle to make peace with God and read meaning into the cosmos did not leave me an effective preacher. Unfortunately for my sons, I also became something of a silent witness for the spiritual way of life. Colin and McLean had little idea of the lifelong conversations I'd held with God, or knew how consumed I had always been by questions of man's spiritual nature. They had been told about God and Jesus and Buddha; they'd heard, upon occasion, their uncle the priest sermonize; they had listened in on dinner conversations about the various religious views people hold; but none of these offered a strong case for making God a central part of their lives. They had no firm foundation in faith that there is more to us than flesh and bones. So how, I anguished, did I begin to lay the foundation now, after being so delinquent for so long in the area of spiritual education?

As I ran alongside Saratoga Lake that day, noticing the invisible wind rippling the waters, an answer came to me.

I had recently gone back to *Golf in the Kingdom*, Michael Murphy's classic tale of golf as mystical journey. I had done so with the express purpose of determining whether Colin and McLean might like to read it, as it could serve as an ideal occasion for a discussion about the spiritual nature of golf. This would provide an opening for a more general discussion of God and religion and the spiritual life. But I had regretfully concluded that the boys would never stay with the book. It was far from a page turner, and I was sure that the philosophizing would baffle them, and the rhapsodizing about golf would seem silly.

But, I thought as I ran that day, why couldn't I simply say to Colin and McLean: 'I've just read a book that talked about golf as a spiritual adventure. What do you guys think golf might have to do with the spiritual?' Depending on how they answered, the conversation would steer itself. But would it? I wondered in the very next moment. Didn't I need to be better prepared to be convincing? Convincing of what?

I ran on ahead, making the turn onto our road, looking over the fields stretching out to my right. The sky above was a busy palette of dark and light blues and char-coal grays. The distinct brushing of the colors held my attention for a time before I began searching for the silver roof of our house, usually visible between the stands of trees in the distance. I spied it, and then noticed that a rainbow stretched across the sky beyond our house.

Rainbows had been our good-luck signs in that golf-ing season. There was the one that appeared the very first time we played. And then two weeks earlier, at the Spa course, when both boys had played very well and we'd laughed a lot together, we'd seen a startling rainbow as we approached the sixteenth green. Its colors were bright and clear, and its reach extended from one horizon to the other. The three of us had stopped still to marvel, and in that moment I was struck with what might have been the obvious realization that rainbows are signs of new beginnings, following cleansing rains. The rainbows appearing in our golfing season were probably about much more than luck. They signaled fresh starts. I may have made a late start in imprinting my sons with the lessons of honesty and integrity, but I had made a good start. I knew this as I stood with them that day, stopped in front of the sixteenth green, and in recognizing it I felt deeply grateful.

I knew, too, as I watched this latest rainbow disappear into the ether that I should trust that I had found a way of introducing the issues of spirituality with Colin and McLean. I promised myself that I would get to it as soon as I could.

*

The following Saturday we played our last round of golf for that year. I wasn't entirely sure then that it would in fact be our last, but winter was coming on hard.

The temperature was in the low forties that morning as we ate a late breakfast. The weatherman maintained that we might see the mercury get to fifty, and the sun was shining, so we were hopeful. I decided to use the morning's slow pace to my advantage.

"I've been reading a book called *Golf in the Kingdom* that's about golf as a spiritual adventure," I said from my position at the head of the table to Colin and McLean as they cut into their French toast. "What do you think golf might have to do with spirituality?"

The only sound I heard was the scratch of knives against plates.

"No idea?" I asked, looking diagonally to my right at Colin, and then over to my left at McLean.

"No idea," McLean said, brusquely.

"No idea," Colin said.

"No idea," I repeated mournfully. "Well, let's try it this way," I said, trudging onward. "What does spirituality mean to you two?"

Colin was willing to take that one. "There's a body that's outside of you," he said. "It's called the spirit. It watches over you, sort of, and it works as your conscience, too."

Not exactly an excerpt from the old Baltimore Catechism, but a start.

"Okay," I said, "you've given a definition of spirit. You've talked about it as if it's some other thing out there watching over you and keeping you on the right track. Did you mean that, or did you mean that this is the part of you, the part of all of us, that has these qualities? The part of you that's not limited by your physical body?"

"It's you," Colin said confidently. "Not some other thing."

"What makes you so sure?"

"I don't know," he said.

"Well, are you basing this on something you feel?" I asked, prodding. "Do you personally experience this spirit you're talking about?"

"Yes," he said a little uncertainly.

"How?"

"I don't know Dad," Colin said, trying now to shrug

me loose. "Why don't you just tell us what the book is about."

"We're talking about what the book is about," I retorted. "Just try thinking about it. How do you experience this spirit hovering over your shoulder? Or wherever you think it is. What kind of a feeling does it give you?"

"When you feel spiritual you feel relaxed," he responded quickly.

He had answered in the second person, but I decided to ignore that. "Okay, so being spiritual can feel like being relaxed," I said. "When do you feel relaxed? Or, maybe a better way of asking, when you want to feel relaxed, when life is driving you a little crazy and you want to kind of chill out, what do you do?"

"I take Jasper for a walk," Colin said. Jasper was their mother's Labrador retriever.

"Anything else?"

"I carve things out of wood," he said. "Or I get working on a project, some kind of building project."

"How about you, McLean?" I asked. He'd escaped this long enough.

"I take Jasper for a walk," he offered. "Or I go out and kick my soccer ball around."

"And that's usually able to get you relaxed if you've been worked up about something?"

"Yup," McLean said.

"Well, I think we're on to something here," I continued, trying to keep this all casual and low key. "That's what I think of when I think of golf as a spiritual experience. For so many golfers, golf is that time when we're doing something that takes us away from our day-to-day concerns, we're out there where it's fresh and clean and beautiful. We're doing something that we like to do, feeling relaxed, and feeling lucky to be alive. That's our spiritual selves coming alive. The part of us that knows how to appreciate, knows what it's like to care about what we are doing, to be there right in the moment, fully awake, taking in all the sights and sounds and smells, and feeling at peace with it all.

"It's a feeling of oneness," I explained, beginning my windup. "I know that sounds like some queer spiritual talk, but it's really not queer at all. What it means is the exact opposite of feeling lonely and self-centered and out of control. When I'm out there playing golf, when your grandfather is playing golf, we feel lucky to be alive, lucky to have family and friends, lucky to have the money to afford to play. But it's really more than appreciation. It's knowing that there is much more to life than just us and our thoughts and feelings. You know there has to be more. You're standing out there in the sun, your body is tingling, the trees are shimmering, and there's just no question that there's a powerful presence there with you. You can't doubt it because you're so filled up with this awareness you have."

I stopped.

"Grandpa really does love golf," McLean said softly.

"And he loves you and me and Colin," I said. "The golf course is just one of those places where he's easily reminded about how much. . . . Just like he is when he goes to church."

"Grandpa is always thinking about other people, and thinking about what he can give other people," McLean said.

"Your grandfather is a very spiritual man," I added.

"Church isn't a place you've taken us much," Colin observed.

"That's true, and I'd like to explain that to you," I said.

"Just kidding Dad," Colin interrupted. "Church is boring."

"I don't want to kid about this," I said sternly.

Karen had been cleaning around the kitchen but now she came over to the table and took a seat across from me. She has an instinct for my preservation whenever I do not.

"I stopped going to church when I was in college," I began. "I thought everybody and everything owed me an answer. An answer that I decided was right. I had gotten this idea that God was like the ultimate father figure up there. He made sure that everything was okay and nothing went wrong. And when I started to grow up and things got rough and I got lonely, it just seemed like there couldn't possibly be anybody up there in charge. Certainly not a loving, caring father figure. So I stopped going to church."

The boys appeared to be paying attention. I couldn't tell if they were absorbing what I was saying, but they were definitely listening.

"I believe now that God is no more able to keep me from harm than I'm able to keep you two guys from harm. You're going to do what you are meant to do in this life. You're going to learn your own lessons. Colin, I suspect you're going to learn a lot of things the hard way. There are going to be things I'm not going to agree with at all. But I'm going to love you through it all. I'm always going to care very much about everything that you do."

I stopped, feeling the need to collect myself.

"Am I making sense?" I asked Colin after a moment.

"Yes," he said quietly.

"I know you think I get overly excited about these types of conversations," I said. "And I know I appear to go all over the place with something you think is really much more simple. But all this stuff really does fit together. You know when I started you golfing and talked about focusing on honesty—"

Colin interrupted. "And I never cheated at golf," he said. "Not once."

"You never touched the ball when you hit it into the woods in a really bad spot?"

"Nope."

"Me, neither," McLean added.

"That's great," I said. "I really do think that's great."

"And a couple of weeks ago one of my teachers made a mistake and graded me too high on one of my tests," Colin said. "I went up and told him."

"The same thing happened to me," McLean said excitedly. "I told the teacher, too."

"Sure, McLean," Colin muttered.

"I did. I'm not kidding," McLean said forcefully.

"What did that do to your score?" I asked McLean.

"It went from a 94 to a 90," he said.

I smiled. "What if your score had been 70, and telling the teacher would have meant that you flunked?"

McLean hesitated.

"You're not sure?" I asked.

"I'd probably tell," he said.

"Probably?"

"I'd tell. But I don't want to flunk."

A very honest answer, I knew, and one that expressed exactly how he felt.

"I think you would tell," I said.

I looked back and forth between them. "I don't expect anybody around here to be perfect," I said. "But I don't want either of you two to feel all alone, either. People who lie and cheat are usually people who feel like it's them against the world. Nobody cares about them—or so they think. But you guys, you should know that a lot of people care about you. You'll never really be alone."

"I always ask for God's help before a tough test," Colin said. "I say, God, don't let me screw this one up."

We all laughed.

"That's fine," I said. "But like I was trying to tell you before, don't start holding God accountable if you do screw up. Don't limit God to the role of the big father up above, or that of the guy in charge, or the final judge. Think of him as being with you, through thick and thin. Just like my love for you is always there with you when you need it. It's a total guarantee—whenever you need to know if somebody loves you, just remember your old man. It's a given. Always has been, and always will be."

"Can we go play golf now?" McLean asked.

"Were you listening to what I just said, or had you tuned me out?" I asked.

"I was listening," he insisted. "You said if ever we were feeling lonely we should remember that you love us and then we wouldn't feel lonely."

"Maybe you will, anyway," I said. "But maybe it will help."

"So can we go play golf?" McLean said.

"Yes, let's go play golf," I said. "And let's make it a spiritual adventure."

"Whatever," Colin said, jumping up from the table.

*

Did we have a spiritual adventure that final day of our first golfing season? Yes, we did—I did, at least. I savored every last minute of that final nine. Pioneer Hills was entirely open to us. We never saw another living soul, though the sun shone brightly, and the temperature went up into the mid-forties.

Everything seemed to come together. On two separate occasions, Colin and McLean yelled over to me with a hale and hearty, "Nice shot." Both boys had their best scores ever. McLean shot a 53 and Colin a 57, despite a nine on the first hole.

I remember, too, that we were walking down the par-five eighth, and McLean had just hit his fourth shot around the bend, putting him within reach of the green in five. He had added up his score on the tee, and knew that if he played this hole well he was all but certain to have the score of his life. Realizing that he'd done it, he pulled the bill of his baseball cap over to the right side of his head and started dancing back and forth across the fairway, shoulders bobbing up and down, hands snaking out ahead of him, part Egyptian, part rapper. I smiled but didn't laugh, because I felt a very private kind of happiness. I was grateful just to know that I could feel happiness, really feel it, letting it settle over me, letting it become a part of who I am, not just a momentary rush of emotion.

I hit my shot and walked up alongside McLean as he reached his ball. "This isn't over yet," I said. "You've got to get this one on the green and then play the next hole."

"No problem," McLean said. "I'm all over it, Dad."

This time I laughed. "Okay, buddy, swing away," I said.

He took a full swing with his seven-iron. He picked it a little clean and the ball flew out low, hitting into the bank in front of the elevated green. But the ground was hard and the ball popped up high, jumping up on the putting surface.

"Nice shot," I remarked.

"And you doubted me," McLean replied, grinning as he bent down to pick up his bag.

God might once have said the same to me. But in the past several years it had been made abundantly clear to me that while I might not grasp the full meaning of life, and maybe never would, I could certainly still feel the full force of the riches it had delivered up to me.

"I never doubted you," I explained to McLean as we walked up to the green. "I was just trying to keep you focused."

The guy who believes in happy endings is going to play consistently better golf than the man who approaches every act of existence with fear and foreboding.

—TONY LEMA
✱

9

＊

THE PROMISE OF REDEMPTION

A couple of weeks had passed since we'd played our final round when I finally got around to dislodging our golf bags from the trunk of my car. As I carried my clubs across the side yard into the house I noticed that a thin layer of ice had formed on the pond. Would a golf ball bounce across this delicate surface? I wondered. Probably not. Anyway, I had pulled the flagstick on our little ninth hole a couple of weeks before. The wind had been whipping it around mercilessly. I had imagined it being pulled up out of the ground and sent flying, a skinny javelin, disappearing over the treetops. It was stored away safely now in the back shed.

As I trudged upstairs to the second floor, the irons in my bag began clattering against one another. It was a familiar sound, but odd to hear it inside the house. At the top of the stairs I turned into our bedroom. On the left side of the room I reached down to open a tiny door leading into a cramped attic space where so many times before I'd knocked my head against an exposed beam and opened up a wound. Moving carefully now, ducking as I walked to an open space of floor near the back right corner of the dark space, I pulled on the light and then laid the clubs down on the bare plywood at my feet. Retracing my steps, I then hauled up Colin's and McLean's bags together, placing them alongside mine on the floor.

I hesitated, looking down.

The boys' bags appeared so thin, and the five clubs in each bag barely sufficient for the game. But after that tough beginning in the golf shop Colin had never again complained about his equipment. Images of him carrying his bag backwards over his shoulder, walking down long fairways, flashed through my mind. He and McLean had covered so much ground with me these past months. I'd hardly had time to consider how the results of our efforts matched up with my original expectations, and had stopped only to savor little successes along the way.

Many of these successes, I believed, were the result of love. We had reconfigured the love between a dad and

214
*

his little boys, an intoxicating but fleeting affair, into the love between fathers and sons, which can be so powerful and long-lasting.

What were these little successes, and what made me think that we had enhanced the quality of our shared love? Well, I began to see changes in my sons' behavior. When Colin went off on vacation with a friend and his family he wrote me postcards every couple of days. He called from far-flung places. He wasn't homesick; he'd truly listened when I said I'd appreciate evidence that he prized our relationship. I knew because he joked about this, which was his way. "Surprised by all this attention?" he asked, calling from a pay phone near the Grand Canyon. I noticed, too, that he was becoming more careful to express his gratitude for the little things that he used to take for granted. And the gifts he gave became much more thoughtful. He made me this little statue of a monklike character, fashioned from some kind of resinous substance. The monk's robe was made of leather, and his little cap cut from velvet cloth. "He is the guardian of the rings," Colin wrote on the attached card, "the forest, and, for you, the 9th hole." I was deeply touched.

That McLean was pure of heart was a truth I had never questioned. But I knew now that his beneficence would be extended freely and widely. This realization struck me with force one night at the end of a telephone conversation. I'd signed off saying: "I love you, Mac." He'd answered: "I love you, too, Dad." Maybe this was common practice for parents and children all across the land, but for a couple of Shanleys, so Irish in the way we avoided overt demonstrations of affection, for McLean and me, it was a new way of relating to each other. Mc-Lean's kind heart and his desire to express love not just to me but to all those close to him, had been at a slow burn just below the surface. It would be easier now to stoke the fire. I had seen evidence of this in his love for his grandfather, a love he openly shared with me.

As my sons grew in their ability to love, I knew, all the rest of life's great lessons, virtues, and gifts could follow. When we develop the ability to love we acquire empathy and sensitivity to everything around us. We become governed internally by this empathy. Virtues become genuine virtues. We don't behave well merely because we wish to look good or be liked. We don't need outside voices telling us we are right or wrong. We know ourselves. And when we learn to love we not only have the ability to give but to receive as well. We can take in the beauty of nature, and take in the love of others for us. When we love, when we feel loved, life's lessons can be viewed as opportunities to grow, not as forms of punishment or obstacles thrown up in front of us to keep us from happiness.

Had Colin and McLean absorbed the lessons in honor and integrity? What I had witnessed that summer and fall indicated that they had. I expected that they might slip up from time to time, but from now on they would know for themselves when they did.

Had I shown them how to make body, mind, and spirit work together at will? Not consistently, not yet. I had a ways to go myself in that great challenge. But eventually we would all get there.

Would my sons assume a spiritual relationship with life? When I had finally shared the intensity of my feelings on the subject, their eyes had widened. I would continue to help open them further. Recognizing that I had so neglected my relationship with God for so long only to have it restored again with greater rewards, I felt confident that while Colin and McLean were coming late to the supper their meal might still be warm and nourishing.

Actually, despite their youthful attention spans and resistance to serious discussion, overall they had proved receptive to all these messages. As these lessons were reinforced over time, I trusted, they would become part and parcel of their beings. Certainly, there was much material for further teaching left. With golf alone we had barely cracked the cover of the rule book. Wait until they learned the extraordinary level of its nit-picking, I thought, chuckling to myself.

I don't know how long I stood there in the attic. The single bare bulb cast just enough light to illuminate the bags at my feet and to begin to clarify the jumble of emotions I had been feeling these last several weeks as I thought about my family.

One day at the end of September I'd received a telephone call from my mother telling me that my father had suffered a stroke. He would be fine, she reassured me, but for the time being, at least, he had lost his sight. A good part of his vision was likely to return, she said, but the doctors would not say how much or when. I'd handled the news quite well until I talked on the phone later that night with McLean. After sharing the news about my father with him, he asked: "Is Grandpa going to be able to play golf? That will mean a lot to him."

As it happened, my father was playing golf again within a month. I know this wasn't any real indication of his ability to see, because he could play Warwick Country Club at midnight and not miss a step. To hear my father talk, the stroke and its aftermath amounted to a minor inconvenience. But this, after all, was a man who made the grand notion of redemption a part of his everyday life. He had made this clear to me on our final eve-ning together in August at the rented beach house in Rhode Island.

For our last vacation dinner, we had decided to stay home and have a cookout. My father and I had agreed to take grill duty, which meant an extended stay in the backyard. Mechanically challenged both, we had been baffled by the intricacies of the gas grill and settled for doing our cooking over barely hot coals. This provided an opportunity for relaxed conversation, and it wasn't long before the subject turned to golf.

"You know that letter you sent me, asking me why I thought I loved the game of golf so much?" my father said. "I did get it."

I nodded. It had been months since I'd sent it. I had just begun teaching the boys to play, and I'd written to ask him if he might take the time someday to consider what it was about the game that had held him so com-pletely and for so long.

"I've been mulling that one over," he admitted now. "Actually, I've enjoyed thinking about it."

I waited, watching him methodically turn the cook-ing meats.

"I didn't know quite how to answer," he continued. "It's tough to put it in words. But I can tell you that there are nights when I'm lying awake in bed, and in my mind I'm standing on the first tee at the club. I hit this long drive and I'm over the hill. And then I hit a three-iron and I'm on in regulation with two putts for a par. I go around the entire course like that, hitting the ball just the way I know I can hit it, if I play as well as I can possibly play."

He nodded to me.

"This is a seventy-three-year-old man doing this," he stressed.

I smiled.

"Every time I'm standing on the first tee, in real life," he said, "I'm thinking that I might have that perfect round I imagined in my mind. I really am."

Suddenly, he raised his arms up above his head. "It's the opportunity for redemption!" he exclaimed.

I laughed out loud, pleased and surprised to see him emotionally unfettered.

"Sometimes it's just a hole or two," my father went on, returning to his customary calm. "I par a few in a row and I see that it's all possible. There is no physical reason why I couldn't go around in par. I think that's what makes golf the game it is. Excellence is available to all of us."

We stood for a time, silently considering our own opportunities for redemption, and the successes and failures we'd had in the pursuit of excellence.

"I screwed up this summer," I confessed. "Last year I really had my game going, and then by thinking too much and reading so much I got nuts about it."

"Don't change your swing," my father said. "You've got a great swing. You hit the ball beautifully."

"I'm going to stop all this tinkering," I said. "I'm just going to play again."

"Good," he said. "You have the gift. Just appreciate it."

But it was he who had the gift, the one I'd searched for all my life. He was a man of great faith. I knew he had his questions, and that he'd looked into the abyss. He told me once about the day his mother died. He was in his twenties. The two of them were very close, "real pals," as he described it. When she took her last breath, he walked out of the hospital and began to cry. He started running. For five miles he ran and he cried, until he reached the church. He stopped crying as soon as he walked inside.

I've been yearning for some kind of redemption for most of my adult life. I have carried so many regrets. I wanted to be a better son, a better brother, a better friend, a better husband, a better father. There had been so many lapses along the way.

As I pulled myself back from that warm summer evening talking comfortably with my father, and returned to the chill of the attic, I was very much aware that many of the deepest pains of my past were finally leaving me. When that summer began, I had been troubled by how I had neglected for so long to pass along to my sons the most precious gifts of my father. I had squandered my inheritance. Then I had become consumed by the effort to catch up, and there had been little time for regret. Slowly but surely, we were making progress against the years of indifference. I had gotten Colin and McLean to the first tee, and could see that their best rounds lay before them. I could see as well that mine did, too.

I reached up, finding the string to extinguish the attic's light. I held the string, twirling it between my fingers. Finally, I gave it a tug and began to carefully make my way out of the darkness.

ACKNOWLEDGMENTS

When a writer who's been at it for years finally has it all come together, he is particularly grateful to those who stood alongside the many hurdles and by their cheering gave him the extra boost necessary to go up and over and on.

When we were young, and he was as kind and wise as I was self-absorbed, Billy Doyle listened to my fanciful dreams and never failed to express full confidence that I would achieve them. He also didn't seem to mind that I required repeated renditions of his unwavering opinion. Harry Booth inspired me to think and communicate my thinking when, during my lost college years, I was otherwise inclined to play dead. Patrick Smithwick introduced me to the reporter's life, and his enthusiasm for his craft and the human contact provided was just the jolt of energy I needed. George Griffin taught me how to keep a reader's attention, while propping me up against the withering blows of an unfriendly editor. I might well have fallen out of the ring. Peter and Susan Grilli said they'd picked me out of the crowd of writers, and it had been too long since I thought anybody really would. Michael Bamberger, when I was in need of reminding, reminded me to write at the top of my game. David Black promised to take me on a grand joy ride and then delivered. Rick Kot coaxed out the full story, making for a deeper pleasure.

And then there's Karen. She skipped around behind me, took hold of me in a great big hug, pulling me out of what was and into what I always hoped would be. It's her love that makes me who I am, a very lucky guy.

© Karen Shanley

Andrew Shanley is the father of two sons and a daughter. He was first a caddy, then a newspaper reporter, a copy-writer, and a partner in an advertising agency. He lives near Saratoga Springs, New York.